list

a novel

list
MATTHEW ROBERSON

a novel

FC2
TUSCALOOSA

FC2 is an imprint of The University of Alabama Press

Book Design: Illinois State University's English Department's Publications
    Unit; Codirectors: Steve Halle and Jane L. Carman; Assistant Director:
    Danielle Duvick; Production Assistant: Amanda Paul
Cover Design: Lou Robinson
Typeface: Garamond

⊗

The paper on which this book is printed meets the minimum requirements
of American National Standard for Information Sciences—Permanence
of Paper for Printed Library Materials, ANSI Z39.48–1984

Library of Congress Cataloging-in-Publication Data
Roberson, Matthew.
 List : a novel / Matthew Roberson.
    pages cm
  ISBN 978-1-57366-177-5 (pbk. : alk. paper) -- ISBN 978-1-57366-844-6
(ebook)
1.   Families--Fiction. 2.   Middle   class--United   States--Fiction. 3.
Psychological fiction. I. Title.
  PS3618.O3167L57 2013
  813'.6--dc23
                                2013039257

FOR MY MOST BELOVED GRETCHEN, NICHOLAS, AND ALICE

ACKNOWLEDGMENTS

I'd like to thank Dan Waterman and all the good folks at University of Alabama Press for their devoted and excellent work.

My colleagues at Central Michigan University—Darrin Doyle, Jeffrey Bean, and Robert Fanning—supported me through every part of this book.

Cathy Hicks-Kennard and the Faculty Research and Creative Endeavors Committee at Central Michigan University were awesome enough to award me a grant, which gave me time to write.

My friends, Kole Taylor and Debra Di Blasi, helped me see the light about lists.

The FC2 Board of Directors provided the encouragement and goodwill that helped make this book possible.

And I'd be lost without the help of Lance Olsen, Übermensch.

I would also like to thank the editors of the magazines in which versions of the fictions collected in this book first appeared:

"Come Thanksgiving," *Rampike*.

"Here's What He Bought," *Cavalier Literary Couture*.

"Then What?" *Elm Leaves Literary Journal*.

"This Placed," *Contrary*.

"Ways to Die," *Western Humanities Review*.

"Inventory," *Web Conjunctions* (as "Years").

WAYS TO DIE

Way one:

They'd been at the depot, wandering the aisles.

The man wanted a new drill, and new gloves, and a tool shed, but they ended up buying a paint scraper and a long pole, and a pack of gum for the boy.

It was almost summer, and the house needed painting.

The man figured anyone can scrape a wall and slap on paint, so why not him? The first floor, at least, and some of the second, and he'd leave the hard spots for their handyman, who could handle the height.

The boy wanted to help, and the man could find things. Maybe some drilling, and hammering, and the caulk gun. When it came time to paint, the boy could spread it on as high as he could reach.

And he could learn from their handyman the manly advantages of the shank nail.

Or he could play Nintendo, or read, and there'd be day camp for July. He would fill time fighting with his sister.

Way one, in the wagon: The new extension pole was tipped over the backseat and angled forward, and aimed, the man noticed, so that if he stopped fast it would proceed at original speed until meeting some meaty opposition like, say, his, the man's, head.

Way one would be quick, though not painless.

✧✧✧

The woman never spent more than they made, so they lived in a cottage, which felt fine, for a while. And then they wanted more than to eat in one room and watch TV in another.

What they did:

The boy postered his bedroom walls and bought a beanbag chair and read upstairs, and the girl's room had all her music and electronics. The woman filled their guest room with sewing, and the man migrated to the basement, where he set up a space heater for winter and a dehumidifier for summer, and his old stereo, and a door over sawhorses.

On his table the man painted tiny metal figures—knights and soldiers and goblins and, eventually, an entire village of hobbits, all of whom he named.

He listened through his entire set of LPs, methodically, in alphabetical order, starting with The A's and ending with Stevie Wonder.

He accumulated garbage—a birdcage, a manual typewriter, a bike rim.

He carried down his laptop and surfed Internet porn.

He bought a bench grinder, and a belt sander, and a set of wood chisels, but never touched them, which seemed for the best.

When the woman came down, she turned one way and then the other, as if she expected to be assaulted.

✧✧✧

The woman didn't think much of mops and scrubbed floors on her hands and knees, as she'd done long before meeting the man.

When they had met, she flinched when his dirty shoes hit the carpet in her car.

And she seemed sensitive to the smallest smells.

When they moved in together, she insisted they replace their toothbrushes every third week.

That their towels be folded in half and then again in thirds, perfectly corner to corner, so the closet wouldn't look a mess. That the sink be scrubbed and then dried.

Before the boy was born, the baby room had to be sanitized to the smallest crack in the floor. Then, poopy diapers went to the lined garbage can by the garage. Then all the same again for the girl.

The tub she bleached after every bath and then rinsed twice.

She didn't let the man wash their clothes, because he confused the fabric cycles.

And so on.

The man never gave it a second thought. When the woman worried, she put things in order, which seemed perfectly normal, and made him a little aroused.

Way two:

This courtesy of the mailman, who stood on the driveway, shorts to his knees, with socks as high, and an explorer's hat like a garbage lid.

He wouldn't approach the house while the man scraped.

Number one, he said: Lead paint makes you dumb as a post.

B: Deadly for your organs.

Not to mention you can go sterile, he said.

Real bad for your kids.

He said, That cheap mask won't help when you get sanding. Not with those layers of paint.

Thanks, the man said, before retrieving his mail, and running a hand through his hair to loosen paint chips, and driving back to the depot to buy a respirator, which strapped over his head, with gas canisters under the chin.

I look like a praying mantis, the man said.

The woman said, What?

A praying mantis, he said. He clasped his hands in supplication and bowed to her. Praying, he shouted. A mantis.

She shook her head. Take it off, she said. I can't hear.

She said, I don't want one speck of lead paint in the house. Not near the boy. Not near the girl.

I don't want your work clothes in the house.

The chips will to get in the mulch, she said. We're going to have to replace the mulch.

Is the lead going to get in the grass, she asked. Is it going to get in the ground?

She said, Ask the handyman if it's safe.

.

.

Ask the handyman, the man said.

.

You want me to take my clothes off in the garage, the man asked.

✧ ✧ ✧

During the school year, the man got up at six, and woke the boy and the girl and fed them, and tugged clean socks on their feet before driving to preschool, and, eventually, elementary school.

Then to the high school, himself, five minutes without traffic, and into his homeroom to start a day of bells and bathroom passes and telling first this boy, and then that girl to get it together or else.

The man lodged his chalk in the muzzle of a metal holder, because he hated the feel of dust.

He put his students in a circle, for discussion, though they said it was the gayest thing ever.

He used the Internet's endless supply of relevant videos, and, when his video projector burned out a bulb, with no money to replace it, he bought a new one himself.

He wondered how many students become teachers because they had one good instructor.

The man liked the kids, even when they behaved badly, even the good kids, who studied just to get ahead.

Something hopeful about them.

Sometimes the man worried that people teach because of a childish need to stay in school.

Mostly the man just taught his subject four times a day, sometimes to the state test, sometimes not, and felt good about projects the students liked, and hated the class for whom nothing would do, and took lunch in the fifth period and supervised at least one study hall.

The final bell always rang at twenty past two, but the man left at five, after grading, or supervising the Future Leaders of America, or checking in with Mrs. Brooks, her arm stained green from overhead ink, a sign of her Luddite refusals.

And he went to pick up his boy and girl, who would be in the man's high school in six short years.

Dinner, when the woman got home. Hot dogs or noodles.

The woman forbade fast food, because she knew better, because she worked in the business, though she never saw any actual food.

She was in middle management and brought home all the best promotional toys, meaning the boy had a wicked set of Poké-mon figures. The girl had many little ponies.

◇◇◇

The man sometimes wondered when career plans became a career.

The woman had known since school that she would launch marketing projects for one corporation or another.

Though she said every company trained you to its own specific ends, and ways, and means.

And she said business depends on people that can put up with other people. On people who got on well in high school and joined fraternities in college. People who could absorb shit from above before spreading it below.

Stable, predictable quantities.

Like the woman, who watched TV at night, without fail. Who did chores on the weekend. Planned summer trips.

She and the man even had the exact same fights about folding laundry and walking dogs.

.

Only now the woman said she felt alone, married to a man with no interest in her, as a person.

And she said that sometimes she, the woman, needed to be taken care of.

She needed him to take care.

About this the man didn't know what to do.

✧✧✧

Every month, they saved sizeable chunks for emergencies, and retirement, and the boy's and girl's college, because time passes, and you have to plan.

If you own a house, you have to plan for repairs: A new water heater. Landscaping. A new roof.

Or a whole new paint job every eight to ten years.

The man had heard of guys scraping and painting just one side of their house each year, every year, forever.

To him, it sounded like pushing a rock up a hill.

✧✧✧

Way three: Death by tools.

You could lose a digit cutting siding, or you might hack into a limb, and bleed to death.

Or you could send a chunk of wood or the head of a nail off a spinning blade into your eye and brain.

The makeshift bench the handyman settled on two sawhorses tipped first this way, and then that.

Twice the man stopped his saw inches from the orange power cord that tangled in front of his blade.

And it wasn't just the big saw. The jigsaw, the man figured, could bounce out of a plank and gouge his veins.

The nail gun would drive a ten penny slug through his forehead.

Maybe the drill wouldn't kill him, but it would make a sweet hole in his flesh.

The more you worry about accidents, the man knew, the more likely they happen, so he tried to play it cool, but that didn't seem right, either.

Chop, chop, the handyman said, grinning. Let's get 'er done.

Yeah, the man said. Yeah, daddy.

The man's daddy had never lifted anything heavier than the pen he used to write checks to the laborers who managed everything around the house.

✧✧✧

The man was not without skills.

Garbage day, he was Johnny-on-the-Spot.

And he mowed a mean lawn.

From that very lawn he scooped dog poo.

Folding laundry he could do, and most days the right clothes found the right drawers, though the boy complained when he found himself swimming in the man's underwear, the girl when she foundered in the woman's socks.

The man did the dishes.

He straightened the house. Vacuumed.

And he could cook a mean chili.

But he couldn't do any of it without being told it needed to be done, and the telling, that fell to the woman, who wanted to know why.

You're that tired? she asked. Or don't you see it needs doing?

Or are you trying to piss me off, she said, and stopped reminding the man about anything, just to see what would happen, and the laundry baskets overflowed in the upstairs hall, and the kitchen sprouted stacks of plates covered in food hard as cement. The grass flopped under its own weight.

I'll get to it, the man said, and he did, but only after the mess felt oppressive to the boy and the girl, who couldn't find clean bowls for cereal.

Or you can feel free to do it, the man said, to the woman.

.

.

You'll pay the bills? she asked. And plan our trips? Arrange the boy's and the girl's birthday parties and sign them up for gymnastics and invite over their friends? Why don't you keep an eye on their schoolwork, she said. And buy all the Christmas presents?

I hear you, the man said. Okay. Okay, he said and followed the dog, who'd fled.

.

He knew he wouldn't change, though he didn't know why not.

✧✧✧

The man had to admit their life seemed to be about staying

afloat. That he and the woman often had nothing more to talk about than getting from point A to point B.

About who would get what food on the table.

About who would get to the store to get the food that would be placed on the table.

About who would get the girl after soccer practice to sit at the table to eat the food someone had prepared.

Who would find another meal for the boy when he rejected the first.

Who would speak to the boy about the importance of being reasonable before reminding him to clear his plate.

Who would clear the rest of the plates of the remains of the food.

Who would run to the corner store to buy the sweets the first person avoided because he or she needed to lose weight, which they'd only manage if they a) cut out desserts and b) found time to exercise at c) the gym to which they needed to renew, but only if they got d) the workout clothes they'd need to buy at the store when e) they ran to get the girl new cleats so f) she could succeed at soccer practice which came before they g) ate the food on the table.

For each other, the man thought, he and the woman had no time to spare.

And maybe they wanted every free second to themselves, away from the other person's complications and upsets.

Upsets about work.

Or about friends.

Or about feelings of being tired, or sad, or alone, estranged from a spouse.

Way four: Ladder.

Trees the man climbed without thinking.

Thirty feet up a sticky pine whose branches dug divots from his palms—no problem, if a Nerf football was at stake. Or a maple onto whose lowest branch the man had to be boosted, and from which he'd eventually have to jump, if a limb needed to be cut. Done, and done, even when his neighbor said he was nuts.

Never mind the bad example for the boy and the girl and every other kid in the neighborhood watching him go up and up and up after setting his beer can down.

Ladders, though, gave him pause, because the little ones shifted when their feet wobbled, and on top of them the man corrected like a seizure victim.

Or they had weight, and lifting them into place felt like pivoting some great stretch of heavy pendulum into the sky, circus style. One wrong turn or tired arms, and down it would come, building speed to land on him, or his house, or take down the fence.

And even when safely in place, those flimsy round rungs against his feet.

And the open space below, and standing way high up and reaching left or right, stretching one foot off the ladder, to bang in a nail or reach a tricky corner with the roller.

Climbing onto the roof and then off, backward onto the ladder again, and down, down, not able to see, a paint bucket swinging from his hand.

The handyman never paused once.

But the man knew it would take just one goof and the ground would come at him like a truck, snapping his neck or caving his ribs or twisting his leg so the rough edge of a bone would shoot out.

That would give the neighborhood kids something to see.

✧✧✧

It bothered the man that the boy and the girl would remember him as old, a tiring, middle aged man with frayed collars and loose skin on his neck and only enough energy to go maybe to the park or for a bike ride but never both.

That the boy's friends would joke they'd never seen the man off the couch or even sitting up.

That the girl would see pictures of the man at twenty-five and say, every time, You look so young.

Not one memory of the man jabbering that his little boy could sit up on his own.

The hours and hours and hours they'd sat outside the car wash and stopped for every construction site, so the girl could look at the trucks.

Or the museums, or the zoos, or the circus, or the summer soccer for little kids, or t-ball—stuff you do with kids before they're old enough to remember the first thing.

Days at the beach digging holes in the sand.

All of it lost, except to the man, and to the woman, who remembered, more, the man's complaints about diapers.

✧✧✧

They'd talked about having a third baby, and talked about it, and talked, and the woman said she'd always thought they'd have three.

The woman said she couldn't imagine not having another baby to feed, and kept their crib and changing table and stroller, and set her face around other people's infants, holding back the impulse to grab.

And the boy and the girl needed another brother or a sister, the woman said, and not one ten years younger than them, and the woman was going to pass forty sooner or later, so they'd better get moving, because no way could this part of their lives be over.

You miss the chance to have your family, and you've missed it forever, the woman said, and the man always agreed, because he didn't disagree, but he never said something definite, or made a move.

Instead, he set his mind on blank, waiting.

Waiting to see what the woman would do.

Because maybe he was too old now for the late nights.

And the diapers.

Bottles and baby food and burping.

Spending hours playing with baby toys.

Spending, period.

On daycare.

They'd need a new home. A bigger home.

How fair would it be to the boy and the girl, having to share the attention?

And they never saw the family they had—not the man's brother and his kids, or the woman's sisters, not the woman's parents or the man's mother and stepfather, who wouldn't travel, anymore.

.

Though they wouldn't be around, forever, would they, their parents? And when your parents die, the man knew, you find yourself alone, or almost alone, or on your own.

You can't make children to keep you company, can you?

.

And if the woman really, really wanted a baby, she'd insist, wouldn't she?

✧✧✧

Way five:

Some old paint wouldn't scrape off, no matter how hard the man tried, and he tried.

And tried.

The handyman laughed and fired up his belt sander, kicking out clouds of dust before they reached bare wood, which they'd need for the paint to stick. Primer. Then, fresh paint. Two coats, at least, at thirty-five dollars a gallon, because the woman said they couldn't skimp. If they were going to paint the stupid house, they should paint it right, so it would be years before they'd have to shell out for materials and tools and the handyman, at twenty an hour, which she admitted was a steal.

Like they'd ever again get someone as good as the handyman.

The hours he twisted his body prepping the eaves. The afternoons kneeling on hot roof shingles. Full days handling a pressure washer wand two stories up a ladder.

He'd said, at first, the past summer, that he couldn't commit to painting. Hemmed and hawed. Said he was busy.

Then the woman brought him a cold beer while he sweated under their busted porch, and he'd said he'd do it.

Said yes to the woman.

Or the cold beer.

The man didn't know.

.

And the man had followed up, because he couldn't paint the house alone, and the job fell to him, and his empty summers, because a painting company would charge a third of his annual pay.

Through the windows, the man and the handyman watched the boy watch TV. Sometimes the girl played on the computer. Sometimes they waved.

Some days they stayed at their friends'.

The man told them there would be other, better summers.

There would be.

The man told the woman he was busting his balls, burning off the paint they couldn't scrape—all those layers and layers of buckling old paint that looked like alligator skin, burning with the heat gun that melted the paint until it bubbled and sagged like chewing gum, and, then, if the man leaned the scraper into it, maybe an inch or two would peel off and harden and fall. Repeat.

Repeat.

He felt sick from the toxic smell when he removed his mask.

.

Probably the mask didn't filter all the fumes. Way five.

Or maybe his clothes would catch fire, and he'd go up like a road flare before he could stop, drop, and roll.

Or a hot ember would start a slow burn, and the house would erupt while they slept.

This last wouldn't do, and the man started hosing off every inch he burned before finishing for a day.

Do you want praise, the woman asked.

It's just work, she said.

I work, she said.

Every day, she said. All day.

Where's my praise, she asked.

.

What do you want, she asked.

✧✧✧

Way Six:

The man's father died young, after the doctors announced that more surgery wouldn't help, that more chemo wouldn't help, that only easing the pain would do any good—and the man sat with his father in the bed the nurses established downstairs, in the living room, in front of the TV, between a breeze that started in the west windows, which looked over the apple tree shedding food for the deer, and the pain was so bad the previous night that he'd had morphine and vicodin and steroids for his swollen brain, and he couldn't wake, and the man wondered if he ever would.

When he did, the man had never seen another man so scared.

Catheterized. In a diaper. His legs shed of flesh.

Waking, suddenly, his eyes open wide, as if coming out of a long blink, looking for something familiar, so the man patted his forehead.

Who are you, his father had said.

It's me, the man said.

Me who?

.

Good question.

✧✧✧

After his father's death, the man knew in a new way he himself would most certainly die, and maybe before he expected—though not, he understood now, before failing his son and his daugher, like he failed his students, by acting as if the world made sense when it made none at all.

They looked to him, but he would always be one of them, looking, too, to whom, and for what?

✧✧✧

The woman complained that the man treated her like one of the family.

Like they were brother and sister.

That he patted her back when they hugged.

And I'm not your mother, she said.

I'm not here to kiss your boo-boos.

I'm your wife, she said.

Listen to me, she said. It's spelled W. I. F. E.

.

The woman said she'd kill him if he didn't go see somebody, and soon.

Because he needed help, and more than she could give.

Who doesn't need help, the man thought, and took comfort in the idea that at least the woman would kill him before she'd walk out.

Death by wife: **Way seven.**

He hoped she'd wait till the boy and the girl were grown.

THEN WHAT?

For the living room, the man needs a nail or screw that will hold the weight of print AND frame, so he checks the basement. He tries the toolbox, and then the plastic box past it, and then the little paper sacks in the cupboard, and nada. But he can always check the garage, where there's another toolbox and more bags of screws. More shelves. More cupboards.

And in one place or the other he'll find a hammer and level, and a drill to sink an anchor, if he needs one. Or the hammer might be in the dining room drawer stuffed with batteries and pliers and a screwdriver or two or six on top of disposable cameras and several small lengths of wire and string. Some rubber bands. A mouth harp. A pedometer. Tea candles. Long, decorative matches. A Swiss Army knife. A label-maker. It doesn't want to open, the drawer, at least all the way, not without some tugging. He worries about getting it closed.

The disposable cameras—he notices they've all been used, wound round to the end, and someone should have taken them to be developed long ago. Who knows what's on their film or from when? Who knows if they're still salvageable? Is there an expiration date on film? They're probably filled with shots of feet and foreheads and the bricks of a building that will forever go unnamed, because only the kids ever use throwaway cameras, and these are the things they see.

Just get them developed, he thinks. DO IT NOW, even if everyone asks why he didn't do this before?

Or at least leave them out of the drawer, for after the task at hand, which will itself have to wait till he's found the plunger to pump clear the basement drain, which his beautiful wife says is sitting in a pool of water, again. It's just water, he hopes, and asks after the aforementioned plunger, which nobody's seen, it seems. It seems they've never ever seen it. Even the idea of such a tool appears to strike them as an abstraction. Plunger, his son asks, pausing, wondering at what some people will invent and others then buy. Plunger, his wife asks, as if there are implements she should never have to consider. Plunger, his daughter asks. What's a plunger?

And he'd give up, if he could, instead of narrowing down the number of places he might have left a long-handled rubber ended staff for unsticking toilets. How long could such a list be?

Because a plunger can't be in the bedrooms, or the living room. Not the dining room or the den. Who would leave it in a closet? And it's not in the bathrooms, because that would make too much sense. At least it wasn't there when last he needed it. So, maybe it's under the kitchen sink? In the garage? In the laundry room?! The utility closet. No. It'll be in the basement, by the drain in question, from the last time he needed to plunge, right? Right, and it is, and so it goes.

And he still has no screw for hanging that print.

But he's downstairs, and the metal shelf with toolbox and tools and screws and nails is right damn there, so he sets aside the wet plunger, fixing its location in his mind, for next time, and he starts digging, wondering why he would ever have piled tools on a box with a lid that opens up. But that's neither here nor there, he thinks, setting the tools in a pile on top of other tools on top of a cardboard box he'll someday also need to open. He can't just dump them on the floor. That would be beyond the pale. After all, he has a drain that backs up a milky soup.

In the toolbox's top shelf: screws, and nails, and anchors, and a hammer, of all things. He runs his fingers through the metal, ignoring pinches from sharp tips, because he has hit the motherload, and all will be well.

Only, now he's nagged by the $19.99 he spent on a picture-hanging tool complete with double levels and a punch for setting holes (which came with a deluxe carrying case and package of hanging hooks and star-headed sinking nails (which, he'd be glad to tell a television audience, really do the trick (no need for an anchor!))). When he bought it, it turned out everyone in the house was taken with the tool, and many pictures were hung for a while. Only where did that son-of-a-gun go?

He finds the carrying case in a minute, or two, and it's empty, of course, except for a star-headed sinking nail—or two. So, really, the tool can't be anywhere but the garage, right?

He shouldn't dig himself a deeper hole, but he does—and makes his way out there through a skinny trail between bags of cans behind bicycles, which he moves millimeters, so one doesn't fall onto the next, which would fall onto the next, and so on, into a heap of spokes tangled around pedals. It wouldn't be the first time.

Then, with his foot, he pushes the big, big ball with the handle over the plastic grocery cart and onto the basket filled with frisbees, which he shoves toward the corner taken over by baseball bats and fishing poles, all tilted together in a lean-to.

He should say, Fuck This, but he wouldn't take his own advice.

Instead, it's on to the tool bench, with piles of tools with surprisingly sharp blades, and the little bits of lumber left over from sessions with the chop saw, the yardsticks and saws, wrenches. The box of sockets that won't close because not one socket was ever put away right. The safety glasses whose bridge got snapped before anyone ever put them on. The six bottles of glue with their lids forever glued tight. WD-40. A coffee mug from the last time he was out here, or the time before that, its insides coated with a layer of mold. A boom box. A really, really old manual typewriter that he thinks was once a home for mice. He never looked too closely, though, because who wants to witness that, and he doesn't look now.

He doesn't want to see any of it. Not the screwdrivers plunged nose first into a beer mug. Not the spilled bottle of chalk line dust. Not the heaped cans of lacquer and primer and paint in the corner.

He just wants the picture-hanging doohickey—just because. And, of course, it's on the spare tire tilted against the wall, because where else would it be? And conveniently underneath, in a small spilled pile, some star-headed sinking nails (wonderfully situated next to cars with wheels filled with air) and, holy crap, some hanging hooks! Which feels so stupendously lucky that he's convinced, for a flash, of the existence of a god—or, at least, the likelihood that he'll someday win some small sum at the local Native American gaming parlor. But only if he plays slots, not tables.

But that's neither here nor there, now, because he's got a pic to hang!

And, really, he's that close.

But there's no wire on the back of the frame, only a slot in a tab where the hanging hook could fit, and the arrangement seems precarious to he who will sit in the chair under where this picture will teeter, if not hung right, and probably fall what with children and dogs thundering in and out of the room, which, frankly, could use a bit more support by way of load-bearing beams (which, he knows, he knows, is a job for another day, or life); really, the whole house shakes.

So, something must be done, and he's off again, and half the battle's already won, because the wire cutters can only be one place, with tools of a certain size, which live jumbled in a milk crate in the garage, and—voila, there those motherfuckers are! And wire? Wire will always be found, because so many things can pass as such, and he's so close, he really is. One sweep of the workbench, one of the tool cupboard, and he decides to give the basement one go, so back in the house and down he descends, and flips through the toolbox, where there's wire!

But it's too short, he decides, and he turns, instead, to the cardboard box stuffed with computer cables, because he knows, he just knows there's speaker wire there, and there it lays, in beautiful spools he unravels until he's got twice the length he needs, so he can double it for strength, and he snips and ascends, to see that on the back of the frame there are no eye screws through which the wire can pass.

He takes a deep breath. In with the good air, out with the bad. In with the good, out with the bad.

Pretty soon, his loving wife will ask what he's doing, because she's been watching the kids all morning, and how long does it take to hang a picture?

And he knows that when that happens, the picture will go back in the attic, to gather more dust, for maybe a year, or maybe more, until he again makes his way up those rickety pull-down steps looking for a sleeping bag or a suitcase or some box holding an ornament someone needs for some occasion, and he's just come too far to let things fall out so.

Well, he's got eye screws downstairs. He's probably got eighty-seven eye screws of all sizes in a screw box split into little squares for sorting screws by screw size and screw type. Only he didn't see that box this morning, of course, earlier, and retracing his steps seems a prospect so awful, so Sisyphean, so much the domestic doppelganger of an obstacle course throwing unclimbable ropes his way that he says screw it, ha, ha, and, without informing the family where he's headed, he gets in the car and aim at the closest overpriced hardware store, because he wants to save time, not money, and get to the heart of a solution. As he backs out of the drive, some part of him knows this trip is a very bad choice.

Because he's not going to Lowe's or the other big box store. He's going six streets up and two over to the shop squeezed back between a deli and the used bookstore slash coffee shop slash knitting emporium. The deli wasn't there a year ago and will be gone in one year more. The used bookstore slash coffee shop slash knitting emporium will someday soon be a new age heaven of crystals and candles and incense, with a back room full of bongs. Or something like that. The hardware store, however, has been around for four generations of gristly, overall-wearing men in need of a shave. It has narrow aisles packed floor to high ceilings with hooks hanging with everything one would imagine: tape measures, extension cords, lightbulbs, and that's just the start:

In aisle three, Dremel tools, and vises and clamps. In aisle six, brushes and rollers and caulks and sealants, and compressors and drop cloths and rags and stain. A little further, adhesives— glue and tape, and fasteners and hand trucks and ladders and letters (for mailboxes and homes and the like). There are vacuums and sawhorses, and sprayers and carts, and grills and heaters and padlocks and fans. Faucets and washers and timers and dimmers and door chimes and plugs and connectors.

And the bins, oh the bins all full to top with nuts and bolts and screws and stuff. Each is fronted with a cardboard picture of its contents and a scribbled-on size. The heads come as pans or buttons or domes, round or mushroom or truss. They're countersunk, conical, oval, and/or raised. Bugled and fillistered and flanged. And to these bins Charles (as his coveralls proclaim) takes him to straight when the man declares his need.

"We got 'em all sizes up to what you need to hang a horse from a tree," Charles says, and the man nods politely, because what Charles does in Charles's spare time is Charles's business.

"Oh. Ha. Yeah," the man says, and Charles narrows his eyes and lifts a cheek, because it appears to him that the man is the one with the problem, and he says, "Holler, you need me," turning back to the front. The man assures him he will make it so.

But the man won't need him again.

He sees a dozen different sizes of bolts that will fit the bill, and they're only eight cents apiece, so he grabs a dozen doubles and forces his feet to a halting half step along the concrete worn smooth and glazed in a pattern of dark feathered to light where others ahead of him have shuffled along, lost in looking. And he could spend a day or two here, and a thousand thousand dollars, or more, but he's got a picture to hang, dammit, and it's time to scatter his screws in front of the lightly mustached woman watching a soap or some Saturday equivalent on a small TV collecting its information through, of all things, antennas that the man knows, suddenly, and without a doubt, came from a back aisle of this store, an aisle solely focused on cable and cable splitters and faceplates for cable installations and cable for Internet and phone cables and jacks. And he almost turns, because the call of these doodads is very strong, and he wonders if just maybe the aisle in question is also home to a shelf of small TVs, and who doesn't need a screen that small for kitchen or bath or both?

"It'll be two oh three," the checker says, smiling so that the man can see a neat hole bored through the center of her tooth, and he's startled back, on track, and out the jangling door and headed for home.

Of course, when he arrives, there's no hope of finishing the task, because the other adult in the house has chores of her own, he's reminded in no uncertain terms, and those chores might actually bear on the immediate well being of the humans and animals alike existing under the roof in this house, which is sorely lacking 2% milk and bananas and a dozen times three other staples, if he hasn't noticed. And his loving wife will be damned if she's going to wrestle two unwilling kids to the store to fight over who'll push the cart or ride inside and who gets to pick the flavor of Cheez-Its this week, and so on, simply so the man can have more free time of relative peace and quiet to hang a goddamn picture any other person would have balanced on the fat end of a nail hammered in the wall at an angle of, she doesn't know exactly, maybe thirty degrees?

The subtext of all this being that she'd like to hammer the fat end of his head into the wall.

So, he begs her forgiveness, tells her he's got things covered, no worries, and many apologies for seeming so self indulgent about a silly little project, and he almost pushes out past the thin ice to say she should take her time, enjoy a little break out of the house—but he's been married more than a few years, and he knows without hearing that shopping isn't a treat, and if she wanted a break, she'd spend the day having her feet massaged by a muscled woman named Olga, and she's also thinking she'll have to put gas in the car, right? And she's going to have to take back the bags of bottle returns, and did anyone think to collect the dry cleaning? And here's the kicker, which he understands, lo, after many years of mistakes: She is already full well planning to take her time, to enjoy a little break—maybe swing past a store with curios and jewelry and sweaters and shoes, and if he opens his yap about it, she'll feel conflicted, found out, and even patronized about her just desserts, and the pleasure will be ruined, along with the rest of the day, and possibly the weekend, and all he wanted was to put a picture on the living room wall.

Which, by the way, he still plans to do, the minute she leaves the house, because he's so, so close to screwing in those eye bolts, stretching some wire between them, measuring and leveling with his doohickey (which will mark a notch for the star-headed sinking nail, from which he'll hang his hanging hook), and then he'll be done.

And it's nothing that can't happen while the kids watch a few minutes of TV in the very living room in which he'll be working, so it's not like he won't be keeping a good eye out, and it might even be fun for them to help him mark a hole, drive a nail, etcetera, etcetera.

However, he's no rube, so no child of his will actually swing a thumb-bashing tool without help, or hold a nail that might could end up in an eye or stomach or, who knows how, a sibling's arm. Because a trip to the hospital is not on the agenda for today. Today he will hang a picture that will be admired not for its content, alone, but for the masterful way in which it is hung so straight. He, at the very least, will admire it for such, and that might be enough.

Only the man is not done, yet, because the kids can't seem to settle on a show, and he can't simply suggest SpongeBob, because this has escalated beyond the balms of Bikini Bottom; because the older child has declared to younger that the shows she prefers are for babies, and the younger child must, therefore, be a baby of one sort, and the younger child, who is, in fact, so far from being a baby as to know that the term Turd might be applied to an offensive older sibling, applies exactly that term, resulting in the riposte that, as a matter of fact, younger sibling is the Real Turd, who claims that, No, older sibling is the turd, which forces the older sibling to respond with the blunt, one word accusation—Turd—which receives a response in kind. And now the man must, apparently, intervene.

Because not only are neither of his beautiful children turdlike in any sense (though, maybe, he admits to himself, their behavior is, at present, certainly crappy)—not only that, but this is not the sort of language that is allowed in the house, and if the two of them would rather sit in their rooms until their mother returns, they'd better zip it, and right quick. And THE MAN will pick their show, which, he announces, will be pleasant and calming and, therefore, something produced by PBS. It will contain, he announces, floppy bunnies OR a talking dog. They choose the talking dog.

He is not surprised. In his house, dogs are much loved, and this reminds him to let his into the backyard, because the littlest one has recently had, to put it simply, the shits, and he'd rather not clean up any more piles in front of a door that, in the little guy's moments of crisis, the little guy can't, of course, open. And all almost seems well, after a minute, when he calls his beasties back in, and they come, lickety split, to get a cookie treat for minding—their backyard business an apparently stunning success, if their tail wagging joy is to be believed.

And the kids are still focused, because PBS has a great good absence of interrupting commercials, and he might just get a minute to finish his first and most important task, to which he turns, maybe even a little mad-eyed.

But the littlest dog is scooching his butt on the carpet, which can't be good, and on inspection the man sees a cracked mud flat of dried and apparently itchy poop surrounding his hiney hole, which is inflamed red and popped out like the tied end of a balloon. And the man feels bad for the little fella, but bad, very bad for himself, too, because his job now involves soaking off that crust of doo and scrubbing the entire area with soap, and then attacking the scooched-on carpet with all the same intentions (plus all the vigor he can't exercise on the hind end of an innocent dog). Only nothing's so simple, and confronting the poopy little man involves catching him, first, and the little dude is wise to the fact that something's up, and he heads upfield, breaking every tackle the man brings to bear, and even the kids can't get him cornered, now that they're involved, and all the associated screaming and trampling feet sends said pup upstairs and under the man's bed, way under the bed in which he sleeps, and the little Shih Tzu is not coming out, for hell or high water, bared teeth in testimony.

The man is really, truly ready for a dog bite, though, because maybe it could distract him from his anger, and he pushes off the mattress, pulls out the headboard, and grabs the little fiend before he knows what's what. And then the man sees his problem goes beyond a butt wiping, because this particular pooch is of a long-haired breed, and his whole back end is a fecal carpet, of sorts, demanding a bath, but, before that—a good trimming, for which, the man realizes, he's gonna need scissors. And scissors in this house are as plentiful as any other tool—and as hard to find.

So, with some regret, the man eliminates witnesses by sending the kids downstairs, and heads to the bathroom, where he knows a drawer will produce what he needs. And it does, and he shakes off the truth that these scissors are used in all sorts of family grooming functions, because *scissors can be washed*, and he sets to it.

And it turns out that the only thing harder than trimming a dog's nails is, well, *this*, and the man's otherwise sweet and cuddly little guy squirms like an eel, and, it's all the man can do to avoid lopping off big chunks of fur, not to mention flesh, and he wonders once again how the kids convinced him to adopt an animal whose hair grows and grows till it needs to be cut, like he's doing, in the worst conceivable circumstances. A real dog sheds.

He pins the little man, as gently as he can, scissors shedding a halo of crusty fur on otherwise clean bathroom tiles. The tiles will need cleaning. After the scissors.

He thinks he'll maybe actually make these toolbox scissors and get a new pair for upstairs. Maybe he'll just chuck these in the trash.

Right now, he chucks a Shih Tzu in a tub, grateful the dog is too small to climb out, and sets the water to warm, realizing he could have trimmed dog fur in there, and rinsed all the horribleness straight away. Or maybe, he consoles himself, searching out a broom and mop, it would have clogged the pipes, which, all things considered, would have been the absolute worst. And likely, given his day.

The simple absence of this possibility, which would have only really happened if he'd maybe done things in a way that never first occurred to him, cheers the man right up.

And now, like a most efficient machine, he sweeps and mops, and then he scrubs a well-soaked dog, remembering to sprayer away the crud ringing the tub.

Then, it's to toweling, first the dog, and then the floor the dog has left soaked. The man decides not to worry about the carpet on which the little boy rolls. Or, for now, the one on which he scooched. Or the other dogs, at whose curiosity he growls.

Because this is the moment. This is when it all snaps together, and the man is delivering the kids a snack without thinking twice. He's picking two eye hooks from his magnificent new collection and screwing them, neatly, in the frame's back. He's confirming to the kids that he's almost done as he double loops wire through the eye hooks, snips it off, and twists the ends into a braid. The picture hanging gizmo works as perfectly as advertised, and with it he locates a right height, and just the right distance from the nearest wall, and punches two guide holes, which then take his three pronged hanging hook and star-headed sinking nails like fate. And then what's left but to hang?

Which the man does, catching wire on hook on first try. And then he levels.

And it looks okey dokey.

"What do you think," the man asks the kids, and they think it looks okay, too. Mostly, though, they want to know when he'll deliver more crackers in the shape of small fish.

"Yes," the man says, he will do this. Then he'll clean up his tools (though he knows even now, when he should know better, there'll be no rhyme or reason to where they get returned). Then he'll clean up the carpet. Then he'll empty the dishwasher. He'll start thinking about supper, after which he'll clean up its mess. Then the man will play video games with the kids, before getting them another snack. Maybe the man's beautiful wife will encourage the practicing of instruments. Both the man and the woman will harass the kids for a full five minutes before they can be bothered to brush their teeth. Then the kids won't go to bed, and they won't go to bed, and they won't go to bed. Then they will, and it'll be time to start work on everything everyone will need for another week. The backpacks and folders and lunch boxes and the like. Then, the man will sit for a minute before his own evening's ablutions. And then his warm, soft bed (after he takes the dogs back downstairs, because they've all decided they've got to go out again).

Maybe, while he's downstairs, the man will admire that picture on the wall. Maybe, just maybe, he will.

Then what?

HERE'S WHAT HE BOUGHT

Back at The Depot, the man bought a fifteen-foot Do It Drill Snake!

Why ask why? He had a plugged drain in the basement.

At home, the snake didn't work.

Here's the thing: THEY NEVER DO, except for plumbers.

So, back to the store, and the same salesman in his goddamn apron.

Next: a Drain King, which the salesman said would pressure-wash the pipes.

And that son of a bitch did the trick. It was like a water cannon.

Problem solved, right?

HA. One problem, maybe.

You own a house? They're a fucking pain. It's the leaking roof, and the garage door won't open, or the window's cracked.

The woman always said call someone, but, what, money grows on trees?

Here's what the man always said: I'll do it.

Like he said he'd get the kids.

Eighteen things to do before dinner, and he was in the van, in traffic.

Goddamn it if there wasn't some son of a bitch parked in the turn lane.

Right?

Some guy sitting like he'd lost his ability to turn a wheel.

Like he couldn't see the big fucking gap in traffic.

Like he didn't understand the meaning of green.

Jesus.

Motherfucking.

Christ.

Our man, he heard seconds ticking away on a God-sized stop-watch.

He heard the sound of the Jeopardy theme song.

The beats of his pulse.

The sound of his own screaming.

Which hurt his throat.

Duh.

Then, finally, finally the guy ahead was turning, staring forward through his big glasses, worried about the world that wanted to swallow him up.

Or so it seemed.

And, red.

Whatever.

The man needed a minute to calm down.

To stop his heart from flopping like a fish.

Which it did these days.

Enough that the man had seen the doctor.

Who patted his shoulder.

Said the framus intersects with the ramistan approximately at the paternoster.

?

Said it's just stress.

Said lay off the coffee.

Find your happy place.

Right, the man said, though he had thoughts, as follow:

1. How about I pee on your floor?
2. It's just pee.
3. It'll make room for more coffee.
4. Which I'll give up like I'll give up life, itself.
5. Which is to say NOT.
6. Because no place is happy without it, you quack bastard.
7. Not your waiting room, with its soft jazz and catalog

furniture and patients petrified from waiting a geological age.

8. Do you tell your depressed patients to just cheer up?
9. Drug addicts to just say no?
10. How about I just don't pay your bill?

The doctor said, If you'd like something for it, we can try Beta Blockers, or some Xanax.

Great, said the man, like he needed more co-pays at twenty a pop.

Though, maybe the Xanax.

Because our man needed a good night's sleep.

One.

Good.

Night's.

Sleep.

He was sick of flopping the sheets loose.

Trips to the bathroom. The kids shouting when he might maybe drift off.

Some ticking noise in the house.

Trucks gearing down.

He was sick of the dog's wet snoring.

The woman as out cold as a drunk. Or pretending to be.

So the man would get up.

Close the windows. Check the locks.

Whatever.

Because the man was up, anyway, thinking about the tomorrow.

Tomorrow, and tomorrow, and the tomorrow.

The weekend things to be done. The mowing. Cleaning. Cooking. The dogwalks. Laundry. And shopping, with the other clueless gawkers staring at cereal.

Groping produce.

Wondering about the expiration date on cheddar cheese.

The price of eggs.

Yogurt with M&Ms?

Or frozen pasta dinners?

Just boil some goddam noodles, is what the man thought.

Add some other shit.

Voila.

.

Then the aisle of earthy-crunchy.

Where our man would get himself some veggie this. Tofurkey that.

It tasted like flavored cardboard.

But the man had his cholesterol to consider.

His weight.

And the vibrancy of his bowels.

Which, you know, bummer.

Like the zombie checker, yawning.

Our man knew her name would be Brianna. Or Chanel. Julissa.

She'd have piercings on every fleshy bit.

One tattoo on the back of her neck. Another above her pants.

Others who knows where else.

She'd have black hair.

Rings.

And her shirt would show as much cleavage as it could.

Which might once have worked for the man.

But his own, sweet girl was sort of almost a teen.

So our man didn't approve.

Not really.

Though he did.

And not just the cleavage.

He appreciated the whole package.

Which was nicely angry.

Which the man understood.

Yes, that.

He understood it more than he did his friends. Their self-satisfied espresso machines. Their Honda Odyssey EX Minivans with Variable Cylinder Management™, Vehicle Stability Assist™ with Traction Control, Wide-Mode Adjustable 2nd-Row Seats with Armrests and Walk-in Feature, One-Motion 60/40

Split 3rd-Row Magic Seat®, and 229-Watt AM/FM/CD Audio System with 5 Speakers including Subwoofer. Their FLOR brand carpeting, and Sleep Number beds. Their flat screen TVs. TIVO, for fuck's sake. iPods and iPads and game players and smart phones and desktops and laptops. They owned furniture worth more than a small country. They had manicured yards. Fiber cement siding on their homes. Summer cabins in the woods.

And what really galled our man?

The towels.

In every suburban mansion, the linen closets stuffed full.

Seriously, how many do you need?

It doesn't compute, he said.

And the woman said, Are you talking about us?

She said, We own all those things.

Well, the man said.

He said, We don't have a summer cottage.

Har har, he said.

Though, to be honest, it was on our man's list.

A quiet place on a lake, with a field stone fireplace.

Woods behind.

A night sky full of stars.

Away from all the bullshit.

Only.

Really.

Once he had it.

He knew he'd be unhappy.

Just one more place to sit and stew, wondering—like he always did.

Bill Gates

$67 B 57   Microsoft   United States

3

Amancio Ortega

$57 B 77   Zara   Spain

arren Buffett

$53.5 B   82   Berkshire Hathaway   United S

Ellison

$43 B 68   Oracle United States

es Koch

$34 B 77   diversified   United States

THINGS SHE DIDN'T THINK

At an early meeting with Client A, in the good conference room, with the project leaders settling into their leather chairs, the polished table sporting a basket of muffins, and carafes of coffee, the woman didn't think about living in a big city like New York or Boston.

She didn't think, as she took a muffin, of a city's good bakeries and coffeehouses whose schedules didn't revolve around nine to five drudges like the woman herself.

Not one thought, though the woman had spent most of her teenage years and all of college convinced that's where she would end up, in some small apartment with a galley kitchen and Murphy bed, it entirely her own, within walking distance of a subway stop and a subway ride from museums, theaters, stores, and restaurants, good restaurants, an Indian dining room with embroidered tablecloths and heavy silverware and bathrooms sporting thick paper towels next to the sinks.

She thought, instead, about how she'd have to explain to Boss B the implications of whatever would happen in this meeting— even though he was sitting next to her, all smiles and confidence, in his pleated trousers and expensive belt. Did he really fail to process these events, or did he simply want to measure his analysis against hers, or was it some test of her understanding? The woman's money was on option one, though who would ever know the answer, because her boss—all her bosses—excelled at hiding their thoughts.

And it was pouring down rain—it was always raining this spring—and she'd forgotten to send the girl an umbrella, for after school, at pickup time, when the girl would have to wait in the wet, pressed up against the school wall, looking for small shelter while the man gathered the boy and made sure lunch boxes were in school bags and homework was, too—before they could run bent to the car.

Scanning the room for the faces she didn't know, visitors from the client's company and a few company employees from their own distant branches, she didn't think about packing a suitcase with only enough clothes and a toothbrush and one book, and she didn't think about taking a taxi to an airport, wandering its wide concourses with a cup of coffee, watching, and waiting to leave a familiar place for another with which she had no ties and only time enough to learn a little, maybe its streets over rivers and sights from high places, before she would repeat, taking the subway this time to another airport to catch her next flight to, who knows, a sandy place. She didn't wonder if that meant a beach or desert or one of each, one after the other, before some next place she didn't think about.

Because who could think in an atmosphere this thick with forced good will and offensive colognes. The woman watched one man puff out his barrel chest as if it were big enough to overshadow the stomach he'd tucked into his pants. Another smiled and patted backs, his head tilted so he seemed to be squinting down at each next man, appraising. And another who followed his short sentences—which must have been all punchline—with loud seal barks. And the younger men, adrift, consigned to following their Alpha males, to see how it's done.

And the women, like her, all sitting, pens in hand, or laptops open, or iPads angled in stands in front of them, waiting, embodiments of one enormous, exasperated sigh.

She'll hear about the umbrella first thing when she walks in the front door, before even a hello or a hug, because the girl has a clear sense of how things should happen, and holds her mother accountable—though isn't the man in charge of these things, too?

Your father could have remembered an umbrella, the woman will say, and the girl will shrug, because—even at her age—she imagines men incapable of the routine tasks, and it makes the woman furious, because isn't that convenient for the men?

This meeting's head windbag straightened his tall frame and began to look around meaningfully, as a sign they should begin, and only the inattentive or truly obtuse continued gassing away in the growing quiet, until even they looked around sheepishly and set down their coffee and then themselves. And this was how it will go: head windbag will make an innocuous joke everyone already knows, but the laughter it'll get. Then his serious tone, once it's time to get to business. A few general words, and then he'll pass the baton to some eager up-and-comer, who will inspire little confidence until he expresses enough reasonably candid thoughts to suggest he knows the score. Then to the third-tier man, who everyone understands is not a failure but is still best assigned to certain tasks, at which his personality or lack thereof excels, and he will manage the PowerPoint presentation and initial questions, until the real men take over again against his fumbling.

On occasion, the woman had seen women in this procession, as the second-hand man. They were always young, attractive, stern women in skirts and expensive shoes who refused to ever look to their head man for support, though this just showed they wanted to, or that they were sleeping with him and didn't want to reveal it in a glance, or both.

Not like her, middle-aged, married, a mom, who will sit patiently and take notes and eventually make the mandatory remark revealing an important detail everyone missed, which after some harrumphing is always received surprisingly well, because it means the conversation has covered every angle, even one exposed by the unimportant observer. If her insight is important enough, it will eventually be attributed to someone else who will think himself clever not to deny or affirm that it is his.

She didn't think about the friend who worked as a surgeon at that most famous hospital, or the friend whose articles appeared on the front page of that most important newspaper, or the one who designed the products of that most famous computer company. She read about them every time an alumni magazine came bragging and begging to her mailbox, but she didn't think of them, not now.

She thought, instead, about how when she gets home the boy will have shrugged off his wet clothes and pulled on dirty shorts and a t-shirt and gone upstairs to tend his business, which will involve a computer game or another, or maybe a book, but no homework, not yet, and he'll offer a minute of his attention when the woman hunts him down and wrenches out a word or two about his day, and maybe even a hug.

The man will be wandering through the house, burping under his breath, and excusing himself to himself as he seems to straighten—folding afghans and picking up dog toys but never making anything look clean, waiting for direction, some idea of whose turn it is to make supper, or what chores the kids need to finish before watching TV, or what plans he can make to set the weekend's events in motion—not because he can't figure any of it out, but because he doesn't want to, doesn't care, has to be pushed along by her, because she is the woman, and women run the house, even if they've been working their jobs already all day? The man was a child. Like his students, who he complained had to be told again and again to finish tasks they would never have set out for themselves. Like the fatuous idiots in this meeting, these cogs in a dysfunctional corporate body.

Like her, she thought, as she watched one of the visiting executives carefully remove his suit coat to reveal a pair of vivid red suspenders, a sign that he was the room's rebel in businessman's clothes. She watched as he removed his cufflinks and rolled his shirtsleeves up and over once, and then again, meaning he was ready to get to business, ready to talk about leveraging the project's core competencies, so they could ramp up scalable best practices and move the needle, get buy in, pluck the low hanging fruit while a window of opportunity was open.

She didn't think of years ago telling a friend that she'd gladly die at forty if it meant she got to be rich right up to the end. They'd been talking about the latest famous person who had flown his plane into the ocean or smeared her car the length of a street or OD'd on something extreme, and everyone said it was such a shame, and the woman tightened her lips in a knowing way and said, well, that person had slept in fine sheets, and had employees serve the best meals to him at a verandah with a view, and the person had mingled with other filthy rich people, who had ideas about some interesting weekend adventure on the Cape, where the weather was just perfect, and the water just right, and the person had never worried, just done what he wanted, traveled, and lived a hell of a good life.

Of course this was before she'd had the boy, and then the girl, and accepted the cliché that kids make life worth living—because hers did, when she saw them at a distance, familiar instantly even in a crowd, the cause of some swelling in her, because she loved them, the boy's smile under his dirty hair, the girl's way of twirling around a room, loved them in a way that made arms hurt and her eyelids close before she started crying at the thought. Two kids so much more than the sum of her and the man's parts, with their interest in butterflies and their idea for shrinking cars people could carry around and would without a doubt make the future *entirely* awesome.

These kids she not only liked but approved of and to whom she could give herself and give and give because, selfishly enough, they were also all hers.

And the man, who, for all his unexceptional galumphing, was always kind to the kids, whom he clearly loved, and who had been with her now for almost a decade and a half, his arm around her in picture after picture as they aged by steps, and would be there for her for twice again as long, if she wanted, even if he didn't seem to actually notice her anymore, even looking straight at her, or have anything interesting to say, or have one interesting passion left. Had he ever had a passion?

The woman snorted through her nose as she scanned the room, seeing people's initial buzz of energy at the meeting's opening sink into a sense of the long haul, and she thought she and the man could maybe spend more time together, a nice dinner out, even some theater, but before even thinking about that she needed to swim her way through this meeting, and the one after it, and all the reports that would come after, and get home and feed the kids something other than eggs scrambled in the pan, and make sure the dishes got done and homework and the dogs walked, and their weekend plans with friends made, and how about just a few, just a few minutes for herself?

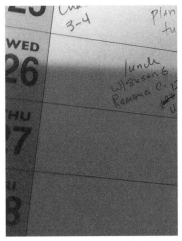

IN EXCHANGE

Because it turned out life included paying electric bills, which—these days—involved setting up an online system of debits and credits, including seven digit accounts and tracking numbers

The woman allowed herself an hour at the coffee shop, alone

&

endlessly unkinking garden hoses, which problem she'd tried to solve by buying a two wheel garden hose reel cart, for $49.95—but that broke, and so did the cheap replacement, so her hose

ended up, like before, curled
and crimped in the long grass
the man couldn't mow over

&

the need to pumice one's feet,
which involved not only the
acquisition of the proper pumice stone but a lot of bending
and balancing in the slippery
shower and an uncomfortable
sawing motion that she always
overdid, rubbing her skin raw

&

an extra half hour in bed

&

purchasing car tires from the
creepy stub of a man at the
shop over on Oak, because he
did have the best prices—but
the filthiest shop, which stank
of oil and gas and urine com-
bined

&

&

scheduling all manner of
doctor and dental and hair

just a few more minutes on
the Internet

appointments—for herself, and for the boy, and for the girl, and sometimes for the man, and for all of them together, and for the dogs, and for the cats for visits to the vet, and activities at the museum

&

shopping for dog food that wouldn't upset the older pup's guts and would be nutritious for the younger animals and was approved by the dog and cat sages on the Internet and didn't cost THAT much

&

&

a little reading over lunch

the expense of a piano tuner, whose work at least she enjoyed listening to, the tapping notes and turning of pitches one hair up and then a half a hair back down, then up, then down

&

regular removal of unfor-
tunate patches of hair from
moles and upper lips and ear-
lobes, and the razor burn on
the smooth skin of her thighs
when summer came, when
she had to shave again and
again every few days before
taking her raw, chapped legs
out into the heat

&

daily medications for her un-
derachieving thyroid and her
high blood pressure and her
low spirits

&

gin and tonic and one ice cube

&

interacting with customer
service representatives who
tormented her with their in-
ability to answer a simple
question without consulting
their supervisor, who never
failed to offer exactly the

unhelpful answer she'd expected

&

replacing the toilet paper roll,
which, goddammit, no one
else in the house seemed able
to do, always leaving new rolls
perched on top of the holder
or just out of reach, balanced
on the edge of the tub—or
leaving no new roll, at all

&

TV for grown ups

&

mosquitoes

&

forms with a half a hundred
questions about inoculations
that needed to be answered
for school and summer camps
and sports but, first, had to be
signed by a doctor or his rep-
resentative and, therefore, had
to be taken into the office

&

telemarketing, which—wasn't
it made illegal?

&

&

a chili dog with cheese

kitchen floors that needed to
be cleaned of the spilled coffee and milk and tomato seeds
that slipped off the cutting
board

&

her period

&

phone calls from the kids'
teachers, which even now
when she was an able, ad-
justed adult sent her stomach
into a fall, because nothing
equaled hearing the sober
disappointment or even qui-   &
et anger of some soul who   massages from Carolyn
witnessed the boy calling his
classmate a J Hole or felt that

the girl wasn't living up to her
potential

&

hangnails, those sons-of-a-
gun

&

the litter box, which never
seemed empty, except when
she took it on herself to truly
empty it, and scrub it clean
in the laundry room sink and
replace, where it was instantly
full again, somehow, and always the object of great inter-   &
est and as equally forbidden
to the dogs in the house   a new pair of sandals

&

Justin Bieber

&

lines at the local grocery full
of toothless locals and the

infirm and overweight wheel-
ing around in electric carts

&

the inkjet printer didn't work

&

the cost of cable, which in-
creased exponentially accord-
ing to an algorithm cooked
up by the most hateful of
souls

&

hauling laundry up stairs she
couldn't see because the basket was not only heavy but
big, and she refused to ask
again to have the man do it

&

their lousy dishwasher, which
was not only slow and noisy
but couldn't shpritz the insides
of coffee cups, which she

&

as long a shower as she wanted

&

one set of expensive sheets

had to rewash by hand every
morning

&

pet hair on every piece of furniture and on her clothes and
in her eyes and her nose

&

missing keys, for which she
couldn't blame anyone but
herself, and maybe the million
other irritating distractions in
her life

&

loud car stereos

&

mice in the basement, which
she usually discovered dead after forgetting she'd put down
traps and always provided an
unpleasant and surprising and
scream-inducing sight

&

caffeine in her soda

&

trips to the ATM, for which
there were fees half the time,
but which she still preferred
over sour-faced Susan who
lorded over the teller slots at
their local bank branch

&

&

magazine subscriptions, which
ended up as slippery piles of
magazines nobody had time
to read before spawning renewal notice after renewal notice in the mail

a little time browsing catalogs

&

recycling, just because

WOMEN'S HEALTH CHECKLIST

CHECKUPS AND SCREENINGS	WHEN?	AGES	20-39	40-49	50+
PHYSICAL EXAM: Review overall health status, perform a thorough physical exam and discuss health related topics.	Every 3 years Every 2 years Every year	✓		✓	✓
BLOOD PRESSURE: High blood pressure (Hypertension) has no symptoms, but can cause permanent damage to body organs.	Every year		✓	✓	✓
TB SKIN TEST: Should be done when exposed or asked by a healthcare provider. Some occupations may require more frequent testing for public health indications.	Every 5 years		✓	✓	✓
BLOOD TESTS & URINALYSIS: Screens for various illnesses and diseases (such as cholesterol, diabetes, kidney or thyroid dysfunction) before symptoms occur.	Every 3 years Every 2 years Every year		✓	✓	✓
EKG: Electrocardiogram screens for heart abnormalities.	Baseline Every 4 years Every 3 years		Age 30	✓	✓
TETANUS BOOSTER: Prevents lockjaw.	Every 10 years		✓	✓	✓
RECTAL EXAM: Screens for hemorrhoids, lower rectal problems and colon cancer.	Every year		✓	✓	✓
BREAST HEALTH: Clinical exam by healthcare provider. **Mammography:** X-ray of breast.	Every year Every 1 - 2 years Every year		✓	✓	✓
REPRODUCTIVE HEALTH: PAP test/Pelvic exam.	consecutive normal tests. Discuss with your healthcare provider.		Age 18	✓	✓
HEMOCCULT: Screens the stool for microscopic amounts of blood that can be the first sign of polyps or colon cancer.	Every year			✓	✓
COLORECTAL HEALTH: A flexible scope examines the rectum, sigmoid and descending colon for cancer at its earliest and treatable stages. It also detects polyps, what are benign growths that can progress to cancer if not found early.	Every 3-4 years			✓	✓
CHEST X-RAY: Should be considered in smokers over the age of 45. The usefulness of this test on a yearly basis is debatable due to poor cure rates of lung cancer.	Discuss with healthcare provider			✓	✓
SELF-EXAMS: Breast: To find abnormal lumps in their earliest stages. **Skin:** To look for signs of changing moles, freckles or early skin cancer. **Oral:** To looks for signs of cancerous lesions in the mouth.	Monthly by self		✓	✓	✓
BONE HEALTH: Bone mineral density test. Should be considered in all postmenopausal females. Discuss with your healthcare provider.	Postmenopausal				✓
ESTROGEN: Peri-menopausal women should consider screening for FSH (follicle stimulating hormone) and LH (leutenizing hormone) to determine supplemental estrogen therapy need.	Discuss with healthcare provider				✓
SEXUALLY TRANSMITTED DISEASES (STDS): Sexually active adults who consider themselves at risk for STDs should be screened for syphilis, chlamydia and other STDs.	Under healthcare provider supervision		✓	Discuss	

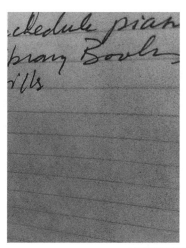

ALLOWANCE

The man's mother meant well, offering money.

Just a little, she said. In exchange. She needed help getting the laundry up and down the basement stairs. She said the man's stepfather struggled with the garbage cans, not that he'd admit it.

We're getting old, she said.

The man said, Okay. If you need me.

He said he could come twice a week. But he had to get home after school, for the kids, and he had his own chores.

And there was no way he'd take a cent.

That's ridiculous, he said.

.

Okay, his mother said. But you'll take money for gas. @80 miles, RT
x $3.50/gal
$14.00

✧✧✧

His stepfather asked if something happened.

No, the man said. Of course not. Sometimes people just lose their jobs. He said, Blame the government. The economy.

His mother wanted to know if he'd get unemployment insurance.

Oh, she said, when he told her. Is that enough?

·

The man said the woman had a good job.

They'd be fine.

Good for the woman, they said, and the man agreed. Good for the woman. Good good, he said. And good for me. Now I can grow a beard, he said. Check out Internet porn.

Probably I'll start drinking, he said.

·

You're upset, they said.

✧✧✧

Who wouldn't be upset?

The man was out of a job, and work around the house didn't pay—not the making of lasagna or the washing of crusty dishes. Not the grocery store trips or pre-treating of stains, the vacuuming, or scrubbing of toilets, the writing of checks, the driving of kids. Not the monitoring of homework.

None of it paid a cent.

And it was all he did.

✧✧✧

Everyone agreed that Tuesdays were good, and Fridays, so most of those mornings the man dropped the kids at school and took the highway west, in the right lane, where he set the cruise and wondered why public radio got the low end of the FM band. He always called his parents on the way, to say he'd be there soon.

The minivan was like a portable apartment, complete with sofas and chairs and a flat screen TV that dropped out of the ceiling. It had a plug-in cooler that served as a fridge. It warmed David down to his ass on the heated seat.

It wouldn't be paid off for years to come.

But its comforts made the drive short, a half hour gone before David knew.

His mother insisted on keeping count of his trips on a Hello Kitty notepad.

She had bought the pad as a gift for the girl, but she said this was more important. The girl would have to understand, his mother said, and the man nodded. He didn't say the kids already owned enough markers and paper to open a Staples.

✧ ✧ ✧

He admired how his mother and stepfather had gotten along without his help.

To move groceries from the car to the house, his mom had set a Radio Flyer wagon by the drive. She used a sled in winter, she said.

His stepfather, who found it increasingly hard to make his muscles work, had rigged the gate latch with a thick rope pull and fashioned ramps alongside steps to the house.

They had installed a plastic dog door in the back entry, so their terrier could take care of herself, and they hired a local kid to come by and pick up the poop, and mow the grass, and shovel in winter.

They'd shrunk their lives to the bedroom and bath and kitchen and living room, through which they beat a slow, continuous path.

They managed.

They were even comfortable.

The living room had new furniture and a high-def TV the size of a wall. It was plugged into a home theater system the man didn't want to know the price of.

His stepfather said, We might as well enjoy. We watch the damn thing a lot. He wore fingerless wool gloves and a stocking cap year round, to keep his blood warm. The man always expected it a meant his stepfather was heading out into some tundra, though he never did.

His mother said, I made him get the good speakers.

He can't hear a damn thing these days, she said.

The man's stepfather said, What, and turned his head to give a wink.   T

✧✧✧

They didn't ask the man to do much. It made him wonder how much they needed him, really.

He ran the garbage outside and to the curb once a week. The recycling he broke down and hauled out, too, in a big blue crate.   T

His mother made preparatory visits to the grocery store, where a bagger help her load the trunk, where she left the sacks for the man, who couldn't believe baggers still helped like that.   F

If you ask, said his mother. If you ask nicely. If you're an old lady.

Sometimes he moved a piece of furniture or got down dishes from a high place.

From the basement he retrieved Sam's Club items that might have been there years: a 48 pack of toilet paper. A body bag sized sack of dog food. A six-pound jar of pickles.   T/F

Insert same old joke here, the man said to himself.

They were all quick jobs, except for the laundry, which the man hauled down to the washer and then back up after the dryer—and that took a good hour and a half, all things considered, or two and a half if there was an extra load.

The man learned to tackle that job first, so he could get it done in time, but it meant waiting, which meant sitting in the living room, with his stepfather, to watch political discussions on cable news.

It meant listening to his stepfather shout at the talking heads shouting at each other.

His stepfather asked if the man could believe the current state of Congress, or the chickenshit way the president was abusing his authority. He asked if the man had heard the latest about Afghanistan? He brandished the remote and asked if the man preferred CNN or CNBC or MSNBC.

The man said he hated all that televised circus and its manufactured issues.

His step-father, in turn, encouraged the man to visit with his mother, in the kitchen.

I'm fine, his mother said, pouring coffee. She wanted to know how he was? And the woman? And the kids? She wanted to know was he having any luck looking for work? Had he tried a headhunter? Was he sleeping okay? He was looking tired, she said. Was he worrying, she asked?

Really, he said. Mom. Everyone's fine, he said. The rest, he said, you know. You do what you can.

Why worry, he said, though he did, every day, and every night, about money, and how his kids maybe saw him, and his failure, as he saw it, and money, and the future, especially—because he was getting too old to start new things. And the money. The stress had made his stomach turn fussy at even the blandest food. Who tells his mother that, though?

He said, This coffee's too strong. It's upsetting my stomach.

.

Do you have decaf, he asked.

No, his mother said, looking stung. Run to the store if you want. **T/F**

❖❖❖

Eventually, to fill time between loads of laundry, the man dug out the duster, and the vacuum, the sponges, a toilet scrubber, and chemicals. He stretched rubber gloves up his arms.

His mother said he shouldn't clean.

He said he'd rather.

Spare rooms one trip, then the bathrooms, and then his **T/F** parents' room, the kitchen, and the living room, where the man vacuumed under his stepfather's feet. **T/F**

Then the basement, which was filled with stuff that wouldn't see the light of day until his mother and step- **T/F** father died and he and his brothers cleared the house for sale—the Hardy Boys novels, and the boxes of craft projects and homework assignments, the Indian headdress he'd made at camp. An old guitar. The dollhouse he and his younger brother called a fort. Board games. Christmas ornaments of Styrofoam and thread and pushpins and beads that he remembered making at the kitchen table.

It's all nothing, really, the man thought.

Nothing, really, he thought, and felt sick at how hard he and his brothers had begged to get any of it, the cheap clothes they'd worn, and recycled bikes and school supplies. His family hadn't been especially poor, the man thought, just cheap.

The adults had said they needed to save, so they'd be self-sufficient, always.

.

The man's own kids had what they wanted. Not everything, he thought, but almost. More clothes than they ever wore. Sports gear. Musical instruments. Toys that filled rooms and spilled up into the attic, down to the basement. They owned not one or two but three video game players, and thousands of dollars of games.

Maybe they shouldn't, he thought. Maybe they needed to learn. One can't have it all.

Things don't always work out how you'd like.   T/F

✧✧✧

The woman told him it was okay.

She said the man would be glad to have this time.

She said the kids seemed calmer, more confident, having him around the house mornings and afternoons.

She thanked him for keeping the house so clean.

She said his parents appreciated the help.

The man said back that she should be angry about having to make every cent, and about getting up early and home only for supper. About seeing the kids so little.

About his failure to find a job.

She wasn't mad.

What's a little less money, she said. Anyway, this is not about me. It's about you. Dumbass.

✧✧✧

There's such need in the schools, the man said to a friend, and it pays so little. Relatively speaking. You never imagine you'll lose your job.

But one day, he said, not one or two or three but four of them had been told there was no more money to pay their salaries, and they had emptied their desks and cubicles and cleared their food from the fridge and said goodbye at a bar after work one evening, where people passed the hat for drinks. The man tried to think of an event that could feel more miserable. A group funeral, maybe.

And there was nothing else out there, not for someone— not for the millions—whose assets only included a liberal arts degree and a clear head. Nothing short of stocking shelves and pumping gas, which the man did consider.

Nevertheless, he printed his resume on heavy cream stationery. He solicited leads from everyone he knew, until friends looked away at the sight of him, making the man feel contagious.

Other people suggested new career paths, that he go back to school.

How about he start his own business?

In what, the man asked.

The million-dollar question, said an employed friend, who didn't care about the answer.

✧✧✧

The man saw the signs of his parents' age:

The pair of fouled underwear drying on the side of the tub. F

Wigs his mother had bought during chemo. T

An almost full, expired bottle of Viagra in the bedroom. F

Lab forms that had a dozen boxes checked. T

The look of vagueness they carried through conversations about the man's smart phone or his interest in brewing beer. At least they asked, which the man appreciated. T

He had often thought they were getting old, but now he knew they were already there.

Maybe they didn't themselves know, the way he didn't think about his own age, just accepted that his knees ached on stairs and how his face looked different in ways he couldn't define.

But he knew they knew.

Only you don't stop hiding the hard facts from your kids, even when they're grown.

✧✧✧

The man's kids hated visiting their grandparents, but the man insisted they go with him on weekdays when there was no school.

They made complaints the man once made about his Nana and Papa—about the strange smells, the boring TV, the heat. They said the food tasted stale.

Grandpa made them repeat themselves.

Grandma followed them around.

There was nothing to do, they said, though the man brought their game players and books, even a portable DVD.

They didn't feel at home. Visiting was an uncomfortable business that required they say please and thank you, and was, all told, no fun.

And all the hugging.

The kids knew their grandparents loved them, but how does that make an afternoon pass?

The man said, Do you see how happy your grandparents look when you get here? And he realized his mother, at least, looked the same when it was just him.

And sometimes he was happy, too.

✧✧✧

The man admitted he was happy.

He was often very happy, when he thought about it.

His house was clean, and he didn't have to carry a date book.

He took time to stop at neighborhood stores he'd never noticed before. Who knew their town had a curio shop named The Mole Hole?

He browsed over sale bins.

He talked about lunch schedules and book sales with the moms picking their kids up after school.

The woman didn't yell at him for forgetting everything, because he didn't.

He was well rested, even though he got less sleep.

He visited the girl's and the boy's classrooms and put faces with names.

He learned that the kids wanted to go to camping more than they wanted a new TV.

The man even enjoyed helping his mother and stepfather. T/F

And they would only need him more in the years they had left.

On occasion, he didn't even feel so bad about losing his job.

Maybe this was better. Best.

✧✧✧

Maybe I don't need a job, the man said, and the woman watched his face.

This can work, she said. It can.

✧✧✧

Of course, when the call about a new job came, the man said yes, without a thought.

Yes, he could start right away.

Because that's what people do, they have jobs.

The woman said she was happy for him.

Is that all they can pay, she asked.

She said to get their cleaning lady back.

The man took the kids for pizza. They hugged him. They wouldn't mind staying late after school again.

A job means security, no matter what, is what the man's mother said, rinsing dishes. There's nothing here we can't manage.

David's stepfather stood up and straightened and held out his hand. Good job, he said. Well done.

And they all meant what they said.

Yeah, the man said. I guess.

- Your home and neig
- You lose all your m
- You know other peo
- You are diagnosed v
- You fail at everythin
- All your friends aba
- Your mother won't t
- Your dog is killed.
- Your spouse/partner
- You are diagnosed v
- Someone close to yo

DUE

Bills are due, but she needs to check their account, and the password won't work—or maybe she's using the one for their other bank—and she can't find the notepad where she keeps track, and it's best not to guess, because three strikes and she'll be locked out, and then no bills will get paid and she'll have to contact the main office not just for the password but to fix her account, and it's not a hassle she needs.

All the little things that can go wrong in a day. The spot of mold on the bread that means no toast.

Maybe the girl takes an extra-long shower, leaving no hot water, and everyone else in the house braves the cold spray or goes without, feeling resentful, and dirty, and—in the boy's case— primed for a small spot of vengeance.

Maybe someone failed to let a dog or two or three out with proper haste, and an accident occurs and then the requisite scolding and shame and clean up with spray bottle and sponge and, eventually, paper towels for the blotting.

Or the man didn't do the dishes, and there are no clean forks.

Maybe the kids left on the outside faucet, and the hose burst, and there's no way to water the garden.

The basement bulb burns out, and she twists an ankle going down there in the dark.

And what if she can't find her glasses, and then can't see to search for them, and she's not allowed to drive without them, and only finds them to discover her keys have also gone missing, and it takes too long to uncover them, by which time the girl is literally stomping her flip-flops in agitation, because she just can't afford to be late *again*, and then the car is too low on gas not to stop, and when they get to the gym the doors are all locked, because it's not regular hours, and they have to run around the building, pounding on doors until some bemused other mother lets them in and watches as the girl sprints to the locker room to change, and the woman walks down the echoing hallway with an obvious degree of embarrassment, maybe even humiliation bordering on a growing anger, because her things might not get lost if anyone else in the house bothered to straighten up on occasion, and because there can be no excuse not to fill up the car the minute the dashboard light goes on, and if the girl had been ready even five minutes earlier they wouldn't have had to rush in quite the same way, and who the hell was high and mighty mother-door-opener in her polyester blouse and a feathered hairstyle from her junior high years to judge her, and by the time the woman settles into the bleacher stands with the other parents hanging around to watch practice, she's so angry she feels sick in her stomach, and in the wings of her back, where the muscles are already always tight as ropes stretched their full, full distance, and she hopes no one will speak to her, because her only response will to be shout, or cry.

But no one says a word, not to her, not to each other, every mom and the occasional dad wrapped up in his or her own spot on the stands, staring at nothing, legs crossed, maybe one foot tapping, staring at a phone or tablet or laptop or a book that can't capture their full attention for more than a minute or two at a time. Maybe they're attending a younger child along for the ride or knitting or just tilting back, eyes closed, enjoying a minute of motionlessness.

Until a thin mother without makeup and brown hair to her shoulders leans back and lays one elbow on the bleacher and says without taking her eyes off the court that the girls are looking a little ragged—that they're going to have to do better than this over the weekend if they want to win, and the woman nods politely until she realizes the mother doesn't see her and says, You've got a point.

My girl, especially, the mother says, nodding toward a player midcourt. I tell her to get to bed, to get some sleep, and still she stays up in her room doing I don't know what. Look at her dragging out there.

The woman looks, but she doesn't see the problem—doesn't know anything more about the game than to usually cheer a beat after everyone else gets excited, and then she looks back at the mother, who she recognizes from other times she stayed at practice. She's the mother always in faded jeans and a t-shirt or sweatshirt, and canvas sneakers. She has small features collected over a pointy chin and an intense stare that notices all manner of things about practice that the woman doesn't understand, but about which she murmurs, agreeing, she guesses.

The time and money we put into this, the mother says, turning around all the way to look at the woman's face, still not smiling. The practices and then what she does at home and the cost of the uniforms and the equipment and the court time and renting the buses. I tell her she darn better do her best. The mother considers the woman, briefly, before turning around again to face the court. Kids don't take things serious till it's too late, the thin mother says.

Well, the woman says. She wants to say it's just a game, but doesn't, listens instead to the pitched sound of sneakers on the over glossed gym floor and wonders if the thin mother's speech was for her, about her, late again, or what if the girl hasn't been playing up to snuff?

She leans back and closes her eyes, concentrates on her heartbeat and waits, breathes.

When she opens her eyes again she looks through the parents on the bleachers, knows that at least one of them has a daughter who won't eat a real meal for fear it'll make her fat.

Another has a daughter, maybe two, or a son whose assigned seat in school is next to the dazed teenager in greasy hair stinking of pot. Maybe that parent over there belongs to the stoned kid, himself.

Every parent here has a kid who's walked through the school halls to see two teens with their hands in each other's pants. Seen kids come back from lunch recess drunk. Seen some boy tear a locker door off the wall. Seen another piss in the plants by the front hall when no one seemed to be looking or punch the chubby kid with the buzz cut.

The woman thinks you don't have to have a husband who's a teacher to hear this stuff. Maybe you remember it from your own years in school.

Not long before, in an unguarded moment, the girl told her how the boys on lacrosse pinned a teammate and shaved his every available patch of skin, all in the name of initiation, and the woman could only say it was awful, because to approach the coaches about it, or even the school principal, would mean she'd never hear another word from her daughter's mouth.

And this in a good school without a need for metal detectors at the door, or guards checking IDs and bags. Where almost all the kids—the woman hopes—have enough to eat, and clean clothes, and parents who care enough to send them to school and to afterschool sports and stick around to watch.

So much wrong in the world, she wants to say to the thin mother in front of her, and you piss and moan about junior varsity sports? Only then the thin mother turns, smiles, points, says, She's yours, right? Did you see? That was beautiful, and the woman has no idea—hasn't looked at anything but the back of the thin woman's neck since she arrived, and she says, looking now, Oh, thank you. Really? You think?

Because, she tells the boy, the next day, or the next day, or the one after that when they're alone in the kitchen making supper that she wants him and his sister to work hard, and do well, and succeed, not just for the sake of it, but because it feels good to accomplish what you want, and the boy slices vegetables slowly and precisely to focus his attention from his mother's advice, she's aware, because she's probably shared it already, and even if that weren't so, and though it's good advice in its own way, it's hard to listen to your mother lecture, or your father, when you're a teenager, because—on the one hand, they must know something, because they made it through their teenage years and into adulthood and have jobs and a house and children— you—and you feel as if you've come out okay, but, on the other, they're so unbelievably predictable and slow and obtuse, and what worked for them probably won't work for you, and do they think that telling their kids how to live will help them actually live? You've got to learn how to do it on your own, in the end, and that must make such a sinking feeling in the boy's stomach, she thinks, that he's going to have to start struggling soon enough to survive as a grown person, without their help, or without much of it, and her little lecture reminds him of that fact—so she changes the subject, says he must be feeling excited about the holidays, which are coming up fast, and she asks if he wants to do anything special while he's got a little break from school, which he does, he says, speaking, words coming out of his mouth slowly, but coming, and the vegetables are being cut with a little more speed but a lot less grace, and it's all the woman can do to warn him not to cut off his fingers.

If only she didn't worry.

But it's an awful world, the woman thinks. Drunks behind the wheels of cars, and careless kids, or some exhausted man ignoring a red light after third shift to t-bone a young father turning left on a green arrow. He was a friend from college—the young father—and his two little kids were suddenly without him, and the wife without a spouse, moving in with her parents for help with the kids and the bills.

She wonders how many people can't pay their bills on time.

How many lose their jobs and then their cars and their houses, their life savings?

Or they keep their jobs and lose everything else to fire or flood.

People lose babies.

Women in America are losing the right to keep a pregnancy or not.

She lost a friend arguing over the issue. She remembers that Saturday trip to the zoo with their tiny kids in Velcro shoes and hair that hadn't yet been cut.

Zoos, the women thinks. Why had she ever agreed to go?

She tells the man about a delicacy in South Korea called torture dog soup. She says they make it by boiling the animal alive, and he says nothing in return.

She tells him that people say the stress and anguish makes the meat more tender.

We're not above it here, she says. People fight dogs in pits.

Grown kids dump their parents into dirty nursing homes, she says, where the workers won't empty the bedpans.

We let drug addicts freeze on the streets, she says.

Even in our safe, little section of the world there's robbery and rape.

Children are abused physically, sexually.

You know Danny, she says to the man, pulling her hair into a tail. Sweet Danny, who's married to Joann? He's a drunk she says, and he beats her up.

What do you mean he beats her up, the man asks.

What do you mean what do I mean, the woman asks. Beats her up. She walks to the kitchen table, pulls out a chair, sits, says, You don't believe her? You want details? Is a slap less than a punch?

She says, You're supposed to trust the people closest to you. Turn to them when you have a problem. They're supposed to be there to help. They're supposed to take care of you.

That's right, the man says, pulling out his own chair but standing beside it.

Only it comes to it, they're no help. There's a problem, or they're the problem, and you're on your own, she says. She draws her lip under her teeth, points at the man. What would you do? It's something big. What if somebody's sick or hurt?

What, he says. Do we need to help Joann?

I don't know, the woman says. Yes. Someone should.

She touches her fingers to her cheek, noticing how thick and heavy her arms have grown. She thinks about the soft brown of her skin starting to fade, and that she's losing her hearing, which is supposed to be an issue for old men. She says, Everyone's got problems.

She says, People think they're safe in their own homes, that it's some place you can control, and what the next day's going to bring, and if you eat enough vegetables and exercise and get as much sleep as you can. But it's not, none of it.

The woman turns her chair, squares herself toward the man. What, she says. You think I'm hysterical, right? That's what you think about women? We're a bunch of neurotics. It's easier to think that, isn't it?

Is this about Joann, the man asks, holding now onto the back of the chair. What's going on, he asks. What's the matter?

Things are bad, the woman says, starting to cry. You try so hard, and still things are bad.

rkey Breast with
Cranberry Relish

with Orange Chutney

h Brown Sugar Marinade

ken with Mushrooms

ork Loin with Fragrant Ga

COME THANKSGIVING

Come Thanksgiving, the woman's ready for a trip.

She says, Let's get out of town.

Anywhere, she thinks. Away.

The kids say they don't want to visit grandma and grandpa. They've seen enough of grandma and grandpa.

Just the four of us, the woman says. Somewhere exciting.

The man says, We only have a few days.

He says, Let's drive upstate. We'll stay in a Bed-and-Breakfast.

.

.

She says, No. She's had enough bed. She's not interested in breakfast.

Let's go to a waterpark, she says. An indoor waterpark.

She says, And we'll go out for a big Thanksgiving dinner. We'll have fun, she says. Remember that?

Tuesday (evening)

She picks the closest one, and they pack suitcases and backpacks, snacks, and a cooler. Coats and a bag of toys. A DVD player.

Wednesday (12:41)

And the man sticks his new toy to the windshield and turns when it commands.

The woman sits in the back, on the bench seat, with the kids. The swaying makes her a little sick. Big deal.

Are we there yet, she asks.

The man laughs—and then they are, they're driving up a hill to a building the size of a mall.

She can't tell if the lacquered and knotted log walls are real.

They're real walls, the man says, and she sees he needs this break, too.

Inside, they stop in front of a fireplace. The kids sit on the luggage piled to the brim of their cart, and she stares at the flames.

.

It's like watching a Zamboni, the man says. You can't not do it.

.

A Zamboni, she asks.

Of course, the man says. Can we check in?

Yes, she says. We're here for water, not fire.

Hamster-trails of heating ducts crisscross the vaulted ceiling.

The woman behind the counter wears a tan uniform done over in patches.

She looks like a park ranger who also waits tables at Bennigan's.

The woman is jolly. Smiley.

Smiley smiles all around.

Her name tag reads Carol.

Carol signs them in. She asks if they've made reservations for the Thanksgiving buffet?

She says, Seats are going fast.

The man says maybe they'll call down, but the woman says they wouldn't miss the Thanksgiving buffet for anything. She tells Carol to sign them up.

The woman is charmed by Carol. She doesn't care that Carol is paid to be perky.

The woman is tired of people whose job it is to be serious.

She says to Carol, You should join us, and Carol says, I would if I could!

You have a fabulous time! Carol says, and they take their room cards off the front desk, and ascend, to the top floor, so the man won't have to hear other guests above.

If that's what you want, dear, says the woman.

Well, the man says, at least this.

(3:34)

They don't check if the beds sag. They don't open the mini-fridge or spring the balcony door.

They don't turn the taps.

The man closes the tattered binder holding all they need to know.

They climb in their swimsuits and flip-flops and cinch the wrist-bands that allow them past the glass to the park they saw on the way upstairs.

The boy and the girl watch their father, while the woman takes a shoulder bag to the bathroom.

You don't have to wait, the woman says, and pauses. Then she goes in.

Always so white, she thinks, and looks up, and then for the timer that sparks the infrared bulb. Instant hot heat. Oh, a hotel, she thinks, and takes out a robe as thick as she is.

Her inserts are made from foam that feels like bread dough.

She squeezes and thinks they'd made good hand exercisers. She slips them down the front of her suit. Maybe a pillow for the man. Maybe she'll invite him to rest his head on her chest.

They ride high and move when she turns.

They'll pop out if she rides one slide, so she puts them on the counter, then back in the bag, smoothes the front of her suit, and buries herself in the robe. It's that big.

What's that animal in Star Wars, she shouts to the boy. The one Han Solo cuts open? Wears like a robe?

Tauntaun? he yells back?

Yes, she says, opening the door. That's the one. Let's go.

The woman says, My parents never took us to amusement parks.

Maybe a couple state fairs, to examine the pigs.

That was acceptable, she says. We'd ride the rides.

I never had enough tickets for the good ones, she says. Or I was too small. It was always too hot. I'd end up with cotton candy all over.

She says, Who likes cotton candy, for real?

She says, My dad could only ever say, Five dollars for a hot dog? I can buy twenty at the store. Or he'd tell us, Arcade games are for suckers. Totally fixed. Then he'd pay to shoot a plastic duck, which he couldn't, and then he'd show us how the gun sights were screwy. Or something.

She says, My mom would hold us by the backs of our shirts.

She'd say, Don't wander off.

You ask her, the woman says, about the time they lost me.

The hallway stretches off like an airport concourse.

The man shouts, to the kids. If we can't see you, you're too far ahead.

He says, That must have been scary as hell.

She says, Yeah.

It must have been.

The fair sucked.

.

The man says, But this'll rock.

The glass wall to the park stretches up the three floors to where they stand, watching. There's too much to see.

When the elevator dings, they squeeze in, down to the doors that open onto pool smell, the cavernous screaming, and heat.

Time for fun.

The man says he'll tail the boy, and then they're off up the rope nets to the rubber floors and tunnels of the treehouse in the middle of the park.

The woman watches them reach the top, where they turn, and wave, and line up for the slides.

The girl is satisfied with the smaller pools and spray nozzles and water sluices and paddles, so the woman follows her, then stops.

Some back brain, catlike part of her can't go, though she knows the water will be warm, and she'll be fine when she's wet under a spray or in the pool, but, still, she only dips a toe into a puddle blistering a tile.

Outside, small piles of snow.

She's the rotten egg, which won't do.

So, one, two.

All in.

The man to her right has a sweater of fat. The man by him has rolls that fold over his hips.

Their puffy trunks billow over their chicken legs.

The next man has very little hair on his head.

Beside him, a man with hair everywhere. His wife wears a one-piece suit that bites into the cellulite above her thighs.

A woman smiling at the woman has blue veins like worms up her legs, and deflated breasts.

A woman guarding the kiddy slides looks older than the woman, beat tired in her flip-flops and cargo pants, whistle around her neck and a Gilligan's all-purpose sailor's hat. She stays under the cirrus of an umbrella that covers her post, dry in the middle of a million gallons spraying every which way.

The woman imagines how much the woman hates shepherding the kind of people who blow cash on a waterpark.

The woman waves to her girl, and says under her breath, Every-one here is white.

It's tough all over, she thinks, and feels less alone.

The woman rides the smaller slides, with the girl, then the big slides with the boy, and they float a twisty river in inner tubes that the man helps them carry up the flights of stairs to big tube slides that stretch and circle even outside the building for a turn.

The tubes are slippery and dark, and they make the woman feel like she's been flushed from a giant's guts.

That's awesome, she says, and they all of them climb the stairs again.

And repeat.

And take a dip in the big pool, where the kids climb across a rope ladder over rubber lily pads tethered by chains.

The man sprays them with a water cannon as high as his waist.

But the big bucket that dumps a bajillion gallons every few minutes—that's off limits, the man says. He's afraid it will crush them into soup.

The woman says, Look, there's a five-year-old over there under it, but the man won't budge.

He says, Let's hit the hot tub, which they do, and the woman remembers when she and the man sat in the bathtub with the kids, when they were little. Tiny.

Family bath, she says, and a woman beside her smiles.

I wonder what happens in the adult-only tub, the man says, pointing at another gate.

He says, Bow chicka wow wow.

He says to the woman, Look at all the clocks, everywhere. It's customer service. Naked people don't wear watches.

And the woman thinks it's easy to lose track of time.

It flies, she says.

What, the boy asks.

What what, she says. Chicken butt.

.

Are you guys cooked enough, the woman asks. Let's get room service.

(10:16)

Later, the woman whispers to the man, Did you see all the camcorders?

He says, Yeah.

Everyone had one, she says. People even stood in the pool with them.

So, he asks. They have tight grips.

In the other bed, the boy's nose whistles. The girl is asleep on her stomach.

People can't go five minutes without, she says.

.

.

They need pictures for Facebook, the man says.

He says, I brought ours.

Whatever, the woman says. If you must. Just not in the water-park. Not me.

Oh, he says. Okay.

He says, You look good, honey.

That's not it, she says, and touches the bristle of her hair.

Thursday (3:56)

By dinner the next day, they've passed the Thanksgiving buffet a dozen times on their way for new wristbands, and on the way to the waterpark, and on the way back, and once on a run for snacks.

It stretches down the lobby, five tables in length, two wide.

They scout every chafing dish.

The woman tells the kids she's going to start with the crackers and cut fruit, then move to salad.

She'll have a small piece of salmon before heading back for mashed potatoes and yams and some of the dark turkey meat in sauce.

Maybe some breast under gravy.

Maybe not that.

Cranberry sauce, at least.

I'm going to eat and eat, she says to the kids, and a woman a few feet over hears, smiles, and looks over at the woman's ninety-five pounds before turning away, suddenly thoughtful.

What about you guys, the woman asks. What do you want?

Dessert, the girl says, watching the chocolate fountain where people stand dipping marshmallows impaled on sticks.

Me, too, the woman says.

The boy asks, Do they have mac and cheese?

And they eat.

And it's another night. **(8:18)**

The twelve-dollar movie on TV features a Chihuahua in fancy clothes.

The kids fight open their eyes, but the girl drops off, then the boy.

The woman sniffs the man and says, You smell like bleach.

She thinks they'll smell like it for days.

.

It smells like semen.

.

She had wanted a third child.

.

She knows you can't always get you what you want.

.

Rolling Stones for four hundred, she says.

The man says, What?

She says, Nothing.

Give a girl a kiss, she says.

Friday

And then it's light and they're packed and out front, the man bringing the van around.

The girl says, Can we come here next year?

You had a good time, the woman says.

Let's come here every Thanksgiving, the boy says. Forever.

Forever, the woman says.

Why not, she says, thinking, If only.

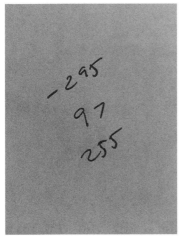

THIS PLACED

Downtown

A counter covered in pink slips and white. A pen, and a mechanical plaque announcing the date: June XX.

Outside, air conditioners drip.

And the drugstore slash soda fountain. The florist's shop. The dance studio filled with girls in leotards and black and pink shoes.

There the woman stands.

Her socks have gone damp with sweat.

She knows that young woman there.

That young woman, who is turned in the other direction. Her shoulders roll down on her frame. Her hips are opened, a knee bent.

The young woman talks to a young man. She smiles. Smiles. She lays a hand on the young man's forearm and then gestures down the block. Is she laughing?

A car the color of smashed plum passes. It has a bag taped over one window.

The car has a small trophy jutting from its hood. It might be called a medallion.

The young woman stops to watch the car.

Then she moves, turning to leave.

She walks splayed, turning out first one foot and then other.

She's had her hair cut and colored. Her bra strap shows at the edge of her collar.

Her purse tugs the shirt up her hip. Imagine the brown of her skin and bumps lit with fine hair and the wrinkles a waistband makes in flesh.

The woman closes her eyes to concentrate on the black of her eyelids.

When she opens them, that young woman is gone.

The Park

They paved the path along the river.

On either side, flowering bushes. Beyond, a depth of trees.

She steps over places where the blacktop has melted in weather.

At every turn, benches overlook water.

A footbridge ahead, its pilings sunk. Beyond it, more path, more bushes, more woods. She hears birds and sees squirrels.

Men and women walk by and run, and boys and girls pass on

skateboards, bikes. They sit by the river, stripped down on the sand.

Dogs strung on leashes.

How many times has she walked this path? How many times mornings and just before dusk. Past dark, with the moon.

With her husband. With her children. She has, she knows, often.

But they don't live here. They never have.

And the path once ran past a park.

It once looped a pond.

Didn't she bring a blanket here on that first night? Didn't that happen long ago?

She knows this: Her hair is hot from the sun. It's the middle of the day.

She has no trouble walking or breathing. Her body feels fine.

Goldenrod grows in every open space.

She knows the boy skating by, she thinks. That boy there.

The brown hair, the thin edge of the boy's jaw. No more than nine, and happy.

She knows how the boy holds his shoulders above his chest, and the curve of his back. The way he pushes with his legs and turns his head to shout at friends.

How he lives in what he does.

She thinks she could see the boy skating in winter, in a rink, in hockey pads and a helmet, and she'd still know this boy from the others.

The way the boy uses his arms to balance.

The boy is waving. The boy is waving at her.

She waves back. She says, Oh.

Oh.

Maybe the boy didn't wave, or not at her.

She holds her own hand in the air, and the boy has gone away around a turn.

She doesn't think he'll see the boy again.

She turns herself and starts to walk.

Strip Mall

Rusted cars fill the lot. Trucks on their high tires, and minivans rounded like links of sausage.

One car leaves, out into traffic, and one replaces it. And again.

She stands and sees an older couple emerge from a car, and from one a younger pair, and then a man who shuts his door unlocked.

Stains and trash on the pavement.

Storefronts of glass in painted metal. The sidewalk fronting them stretches a half-mile. Small squares of gravel shelter saplings fixed by wires.

A bicycle rack.

A garbage can.

Parking signs.

She walks, looking in each window, wondering why she's here.

Not to buy a cell phone. Or a sandwich. Or a haircut. She's not here to frame a painting or a photo.

Not to buy a book. Not to buy computer parts.

She doesn't need to mail a package.

She does not want a cold drink.

A woman walks to the parking lot with a package she sets down before opening her car door.

She hasn't seen this woman before.

Blue veins mark this woman's legs. She has white skin on her heels. Long shorts with pockets. A purse on a strap. Thin, stiff hair the woman can't imagine owning.

The woman pulls the purse off her shoulder, lifts the package, which isn't a package, at all. It's a little girl, maybe five, with long, light brown hair—a little girl with baby fat arms.

The little girl shouldn't need lifting into the car, but she won't go on her own. She doesn't want to, the woman thinks.

The face she makes. Her folded arms.

She has red juice around her mouth.

She wears dirty pants a size too small and a necklace of plastic beads over her shirt.

How beautiful she is.

She can't belong to this woman who shuts the car door too hard.

The woman should say something.

She wonders why they don't see her watching?

She wonders if she could open the passenger's door and ask to go.

Store

The scuffed linoleum floors. The carts on bad wheels.

Managers in the elevated office.

The gumball machines by the automatic doors.

Racks of candy and toenail clippers in the checkout aisles.

The produce. The meat cases.

Shelves and shelves of eggs.

Old people at tables by the bakery, drinking coffee. The men wear ironed pants. The women watch the shoppers.

Workers in matching clothes, and workers in smocks behind counters, and workers fixing flowers.

The pharmacist has a white coat.

Swinging doors that open onto the back rooms.

The dirty bathrooms up front.

Chickens rotating on spits at the deli. That smell.

Freezer after freezer on the floor, open like trenches. Others upright behind fogging glass.

Aisles with cereal. Aisles with cans of tomatoes. Aisles with birdseed and bleach.

The customers trolling the shelves, picking items for their carts.

That man the next aisle over. That bearded man in his sweater, handling cans. That man doesn't seem to have a thought. Look at him relax into his shoes, humming. He can't imagine someone watching him. He doesn't seem worried or sad or guilty.

He's never done a thing wrong.

He's never cheated on a test.

Never stolen a pack of gum.

Never walked on a bill.

Not him. Not that man.

He never emptied out another man's life.

Well then who did?

She uncurls an index finger into a question and thinks. Then she points.

Maybe it is that guy.

The Stylist's Shop

Like every other stylist's shop ever, chairs spinning on fat poles alongside a counter with jars of blue fluid and combs and clippers and dryers for hair.

The TV showing reruns.

Seats filled with women watching, men reading magazines.

The snap of the capes. Hair on the floor. Talcum.

When she steps in the room goes still.

They seem to know her here.

How?

The barber nods and the pace of the place catches again.

What do they know?

The Restaurant

The table has one short leg. The red and white plastic tablecloth. A plate with a rolled napkin on top. A fork, a knife, a spoon. Slatted blinds over the window.

A counter by the back, its bell and spinning ring of slips.

That woman again. That woman who walks splayed. Maybe the woman knows her from here.

Maybe the woman comes here because she knows her.

That woman's a waitress, but not hers. She doesn't look her way.

The woman wants her to look. She wants to see how her teeth sit forward to catch her lip.

The woman wants to see the hair touching her neck.

That woman has the smallest wrinkles in the skin by her eyes.

The woman thinks she must smell of food, and clothes that have been worn all day.

To the waiter who comes to the table, the woman says she's

here to eat supper. She says she'll have some of this, and a piece of that, and a drink.

That woman walks through a door to the rear and doesn't come back.

Outside Town

She drives and drives past houses stretched like lights along the road. She passes fields filled with mud and cows. She passes stands of trees. She smells wood smoke and thinks she could go on like this, slipping out of one place into another. She can barely steer for the sun in her eyes.

Home

A room. A yellow sofa on casters.

Carpeting.

And another room, its table covered in mail still sealed and circulars and plastic cups.

In the kitchen, a full glass under the dripping tap.

A new mouse in a trap she puts gently in the trash.

The bathroom with black and white checkered tile. A rusted medicine cabinet with a slot for razor blades. A shower stall, its plastic floor sunk like the peeled end of an egg.

She goes to the bedroom and lays down.

On the dresser two belts. In the closet, skirts. A pair of boots on the floor.

Above her head a window with one sheer curtain.

The window is closed.

She lies on the bed on her back in her clothes.

She doesn't have a book to read.

The clock by the bed is only a clock.

There's no TV.

She folds her hands on her chest. She feels her heart turn.

She feels the solid wall of her ribs.

The unbroken bones of her fingers.

The covering skin.

She's uninjured.

Healthy.

Some would say lucky.

People have said it.

That she lives.

With barely a scratch.

.

Only she doesn't feel it.

She doesn't feel lucky.

Not lucky.

She only feels awake.

And she can leave her eyes open.

Or she can close them.

Open.

Closed.

It won't make a difference.

There's nothing to see here.

Josh
Sydney
Laura
Laura M
Anna
~~James~~
James

SHRINK

Fine, I said.

I meant it.

We were ready to try something else.

So, here we are.

I mean, I'm here, and she's there.

✧

I said some unkind things.

I'm too embarrassed to repeat them.

She declared our discussion at an end.

Fuck you, she said.

.

Well, then. Fuck you, too.

✧

She pointed at the door.

I waited till I found a house to rent.

I slept in our bed, and used our bathroom, and cooked dinner, like always.

I told the kids at the end of the month.

They knew, already, and they understood.

That's what they said.

Only no one told them I was taking the old dog, because three was too many for their mom.

That caused a fuss.

✧

He was their dog, they said.

They picked him out.

Raised him.

They couldn't remember not having him.

Their entire lives.

And we're not talking about little kids here.

My girl is so tall.

My boy almost old enough to drive.

That's a long time to have a dog.

Such a good boy.

And he's coming with me, their father.

I've known them even longer.

✧

Of course I get it.

The dog never argued with their mother.

He didn't make anyone do chores or go to their rooms.

He never punched a wall.

He's a gentle beast.

I like him better than me. By a lot.

✧

Anyway, it's apples and oranges.

They'll miss me, too.

It's what they said.

✧

What happened between my wife and me?

That's a tough question.

Here's an answer:

We never went out, even when we could.

At home, she took her friends' phone calls, while I went upstairs to watch TV.

Does that explain it?

✧

The kids helped me move.

We packed boxes, and I rented a van for the weekend.

We hauled stuff down the front steps of the house and back up new ones at my place.

Their mother didn't like it, but I wanted them involved.

I wanted them to know it was just a few miles over.

I let them pick bedrooms.

I put myself in the one left over.

We ate pizza on the floor.

We settled on one of the Rocky films, or part of it.

The kids wanted to head home halfway through.

They said they'd be able to sleep without seeing Sly win the final fight.

I was glad they could sleep.

✧

Me, I was back to the futon and frame.

A kitchen with bubbled linoleum.

A yellow stove.

Empty walls with nail holes.

Dust.

Whatever that smell is.

Pizza.

Chinese food.

Unfolded clothes.

Beer every night.

Being alone.

Feeling very bad.

✧

To be honest, I already drank beer every night.

✧

Now I wake and walk the dog.

I make coffee.

Eat toast.

Listen to the radio.

Drive to work, like always.

Exchange a few words with my colleagues.

They all know.

They look at me these days.

They don't say a thing.

I work.

Grab takeout on the way home.

Walk the dog.

Turn on the TV for the noise.

Go on the Internet.

Maybe read.

Hit the hay.

Think about the new noises here.

The asthmatic furnace.

Creaking ceilings.

Chimes on the neighbor's porch.

Eventually, sleep.

Repeat.

✧

Then there's everything else.

My boy phoned because his sister called him a turd, and his mother didn't want to hear it.

And their mother wanted to talk to me, because the kids couldn't drive themselves to practice, and she couldn't be two places at once.

No plans had been made.

Be prepared for my calls, she said.

I said I didn't know what I'd do without them.

.

She passed the phone to my boy, who asked, again, why he couldn't move with me, and the dog.

I said he knew why.

Though he and his sister were always welcome, anytime.

But he should stop asking to move.

He would hurt his mother's feelings.

I figured that was the point.

✧

Add to my days:
Driving the boy to hockey.
And swimming for my girl.
Piano lessons.
Choir.
Rides after yearbook.
After school newspaper meetings.
From the library.
To movies with their friends.
Parties.
Weeknight games.

Games on weekends.

Fundraising events.

It seems like a lot.

It is.

Thank god.

✧

This is not about a new life.

This is not about a low slung car.

Not about nights out with my great, new friends.

I don't want any great, new friends.

I'm not looking to lose weight.

I don't want a new hairstyle, or new clothes.

I don't need a hobby. TV is just fine.

I don't want a vibrant, young girlfriend filled with joie de vivre.

God, no.

The thought makes me want to nap.

I was young.

Now I'm not.

Now I have a job I like.

I love my kids.

I have a good dog.

I'm plenty busy.

I just didn't want to fight with my wife.

✧

Ex-wife?

✧

I don't know if we'll file for divorce.

It seems like a pain.

Expensive.

And another thing to fight about.

So, why bother?

It would involve outside parties.

She and I don't have use for that.

Their dumb ideas.

We never had luck with marriage counselors.

Maybe they made some sense.

About that she and I couldn't agree.

The best one modeled kindness.

Compassion.

It rubbed off, which helped, for a while.

That was not dumb.

That was good.

We won't get compassion from lawyers, though.

It's not their thing.

✧

The kids want to know where things stand.

"Separation" doesn't suit them.

They ask, Are you getting divorced, or not?

As if knowing will help.

As if things can be yes or no.

They think that knowing helps you move ahead.

And I want to ask:

Move ahead where?

To what end?

Why?

I don't ask.

They'd probably answer.

Or try to.

Teenagers.

✧

The kids sleep late.

I used to go to their rooms three, four times.

I'd say it's time to get up.

Eventually, I threatened.

Of course, that was then.

They don't spend many weekdays here.

They're here on weekends.

On weekends, forget about it. They sleep till nine or ten.

They drift out to eat cereal, watch TV.

I ask about school.

Maybe I make them straighten up a bit.

It's not a hotel, after all.

Sometimes my sweet girl asks if I want to make cookies.

Then we do.

Sometimes we stop at the store to buy contact lens solution or a hair clasp.

The boy wants to know again and again who builds a house with no fireplace.

I ask about their mother, and they look at me.

We eat takeout, watch TV.

Saturday, Sunday.

They hug the dog, and me, if I insist.

And they go home.

✧

When kids are little, they get up at five or six.

They shout for you, or come climb in your bed.

And then you're up, and you're tired.

You're always tired raising kids.

You're always raising them.

Kids need to be washed and watched and fed and changed.

They need someone to play with.

They need to learn to be nice to the dog.

For us, it was rule number one:

Always be nice to the dog.

And all of it starts at an unholy hour.

Though the kids don't think so.

They're ready to watch TV.

Spill marbles.

Maybe they just chase each other, screaming, because.

This is what they do.

But they grow.

And you wake them, because, all of a sudden, all they want is sleep.

But you've been up early for a decade or so.

Now, you always wake early.

And you've been up for hours.

✧

And I have work.

And the dog is always home.

I'm not lonely.

.

But I do miss my wife

.

There's no one to tell about the traffic.

Or why I didn't have time for lunch.

I don't get to hear what she plans to do tomorrow.

Why she's pissed at her friend.

Nobody reminds me to take my vitamins.

Or to stop eating before I feel sick.

No one kisses me when I walk in the door, or out.

Except the dog.

There's no company walking the dog.

Never a good morning or a good night.

Or a thanks for some small gift.

Or some small gift.

Then, again.

I've been missing my wife for years.

✧

It's the little shit that makes life hard.

All the cleaning of bathrooms.

Shopping again and again for milk and bread.

Mowing the lawn.

The house needing paint.

Oil changes.

The credit card bill.

Making lunches.

Buying clothes and washing clothes and folding clothes.

That junk piled in the garage.

Shrubs.

Our broken sofa.

Scrambled eggs for supper, again.

But how could we complain?

We knew that if these were the worst of our problems, we should feel lucky.

We didn't.

✧

My buddy, Robert, flies model planes.

My in-laws buy trinkets and gew gaws to give their grandkids.

At work, people plan vacations, take them, and talk about the fun.

They have dinner parties.

They talk about yard work and projects around the house.

They own horses, snowmobiles, cabins by lakes.

Sometimes they go to cities to see concerts or museums.

One man takes nature photos.

A woman tells us about her yoga.

Another about crossfit.

They seem healthy, happy.

.

I drink beer and watch TV. Read crumpled magazines on the toilet. Surf the Internet.

I'm a bummer.

✧

I write these.

And it's not nothing, though no one reads them.

It gives me a chance to think.

Which I didn't when I lived at home.

Now I live alone.

Doing some thinking.

To some end.

I should sit cross-legged in front of the TV, rubbing my Buddha belly.

To seekers, I will offer wisdom.

I will direct them to the dog at my side.

I will say, Look at the simplicity of his being. He breathes and wags his tail. He eats and poops and wants a walk.

He is.

Ha.

Maybe, instead, I'll learn a little about myself.

Maybe make something of the rest of my life.

✧

I've got maybe thirty years.

Then a rapid decline.

Death.

What do you do with thirty years, maybe less?

People say they'll travel, but they don't.

They say they'll relax, enjoy the little things.

Take up hiking.

Volunteer with those in need.

They don't.

They don't move to Mexico.

They don't spend more time gardening, taking classes.

They don't enjoy lunches out.

They don't experiment with pottery or yoga.

Do they take that cruise?

Do they winter in Florida?

Do they buy the sports car?

No, they don't.

They get swollen veins in the ass.

Rotten teeth and gums.

End up covered in lumps, benign and other.

With clogged veins.

Cloudy eyes.

And flopping heart flaps.

A uterus that needs removal.

Or a breast. Or both.

A prostate.

They stay home, and up late, watching TV.

And they get up late, and eat lunch at the local grocery store.

Then they go home, and watch TV.

They worry about money.

They watch TV.

They attend the funerals of their friends.

They wait for their kids to call.

And wait.

Right?

They don't become happy, or enlightened.

They become resigned and ready to die.

✧

Me, I'll always drive downtown for fondue.

Eat foods stuffed with hot peppers.

I'll camp in the woods.

Ski.

Sit in the sunny seats at the baseball game.

Travel to Cairo.

I'll do it with my kids, when I can.

Then my grandkids.

Who I'll play with on the floor.

Or in the sandbox.

Or the pool.

That sickly guy in the baggy trunks.

Who's gonna care?

.

I'll keep working, make money.

I'll give it to my kids.

They'll need it to buy houses.

And so on.

And so forth.

.

Then, a massive stroke, I hope.

Or a massive coronary.

Something massive.

✧

My sweet dog has only a few years left.

He's gray on his muzzle.

He's gotten chubby and slow.

He sleeps a lot, or sits in the yard, watching.

Mostly, he doesn't bother to bark at what he sees.

Sometimes he can't quite manage the stairs.

The other day I found him stuck halfway, too scared to move.

I took him to the sofa, and we sat.

And I thought about this sweet boy with us every day, all day, every week of every month for twelve years.

Now, it's just him and me.

Pretty soon, just me.

Maybe I cried a little.

I'm not ashamed to admit it.

✧

Sometimes I wonder about my wife and me.

What it would take to fix our mess.

I could call and ask her to lunch.

She'd think the worst.

She'd want to know why we couldn't talk on the phone.

She'd want to know my angle.

She'd think I want the kids.

That I've got a lawyer telling me to pressure.

Then sue for custody.

This is what a lawyer would say.

But that's not why I would call.

I'd call about a calm meal complete with a small salad and maybe a cup of soup.

A sandwich.

Two people sitting down for a conversation.

Something civil, even friendly?

Two people with a long history trying to make things right.

I haven't called, and I won't.

She hates the phrase, "make things right."

What does that mean, she'd say. What things?

She'd say, You think there's a right and a wrong?

And our argument would start.

✧

How do people say it?

We didn't always fight?

My wife and I did.

I don't mean fight fight.

I mean argue, disagree.

We discussed things in a heated manner.

We discussed the value of entitlements to traditionally disenfranchised peoples.

The problems inherent in our culture's turn to a visual knowledge.

To us it seemed thoughtful.

And by that I mean full of thought.

Only it got ugly.

As if the point was to win.

✧

Because we started arguing about whether chocolate beats vanilla.

About the number of minutes needed to boil an egg.

How much dishwasher detergent to use.

The right way to park.

It was not charming or cute.

I was not Harry.

She was not Sally.

We got goddamn angry.

Relentless.

Then that's all it was.

We had no patience for a puddle on the bathroom floor.

Or coffee grounds in the sink.

Some days we woke up mad.

Went to bed the same way.

It was awful.

Unreasonable.

Dysfunctional.

And before we even had kids.

✧

Then we had kids.

Babies are a lot of work. I've said this.

There's a lot of feeding. Rocking. Bathing.

There's not a lot of sleep.

There's the buying of clothes. The making of meals. The cleaning up after.

After a couple years, potty training.

Training them not to bite.

It's just as hard when they start school. Then there's homework, too.

Later, when they're ten, you drive them places. Help them with sports. And choir. It's a lot of work.

Do I even need to say that teenagers, they're a lot of work? Even just at the start?

Even the best parents, in the face of it all, they might feel stretched thin. Put upon. They might bicker.

.

My wife and I almost traded punches.

✧

.
She can never be angry with the kids.

They can spill or fight or talk back. Break things. Leave underwear on the living room floor.

Dawdle.

Disobey.

They can make bedtime hard. Get in trouble at school. Watch TV they shouldn't.

Be rude about supper.

Make a mess of their rooms.

All that and more, and you could see the anger coming off my sweet wife like air over hot blacktop.

And she'd find a reason to yell at me.

She sternly instructed the kids. Presented consequences.

Me, I got screamed at because I left the toilet seat up.

✧

I mean, I didn't want her to yell at the kids, either.

They're just kids.

But she didn't have to let it loose on me.

And the look she'd get.

Like she smelled a smell.

I didn't even have to speak.

Just walk in the room.

✧

And I took things out on her.

I got impatient that she'd lost her keys, or stayed on the phone forever, or made noodles again.

I hate noodles.

I mean, I was annoyed. Maybe I glowered. She said I glowered.

Sometimes I made a comment.

Maybe I yelled.

Who doesn't?

Then I got yelled at for yelling, which, she said, was ugly, and extremely unkind.

So, I stopped.

But, by then, I had a history.

And she felt upset each time her keys went missing.

She was afraid I would yell.

Again.

Yes.

I got in trouble because I was glowering inside.

Which, you know, was entirely true.

But what the hell was I supposed to do?

✧

Sometimes, we could put our anger aside.

We learned to say, That makes me feel upset because.

We asked, politely, I'm wondering why you didn't buy lettuce.

It was good for the kids.

Those times.

They walked less like watching for land mines.

But they knew.

It couldn't last.

Work puts on pressure, or you have car insurance to pay, or the spigot in back of the house cracks, flooding the basement.

And everything goes to shit.

✧

Then the straw that broke the camel's back.

And I said some unkind things.

✧

I yelled at the kids, too.

Yelled because they wouldn't stop horsing around.

Because they wouldn't stop bickering.

Because they didn't do their homework.

Didn't mow the lawn.

Because they sat forever in front of the goddamn TV.

Because they left a potato chip bag in reach of the dogs.

I yelled at them because they talked back.

Because they disobeyed curfew.

Lost an expensive cell phone.

Left the toilet paper holder bare.

I yelled at them a lot, I guess.

I still do.

But there's yelling, and there's yelling.

And I never really, really yelled at them.

Not like I did at my wife.

I mean, she was right about the ugliness.

Sometimes I wished her dead.

✧

People at work say I should head out for a drink. There's always one group or another going to happy hour.

Or my friend, Andy, has tickets to a game.

My mother calls every weekend, like she and my stepfather used to, when I was in college.

.

I believe the people at work don't care if I come.

And Andy says it's my loss, but he leaves it at that.

They're just being decent.

The divorced dad—for all they know—can't bear his empty house. Maybe he weeps himself to sleep. Maybe there's a rope ready in the garage.

They don't know, because I don't say, and I won't.

Maybe I've let something slip to Andy, over a beer, but nothing I remember or regret.

One eventually learns not to share much.

That causes more problems.

I mean, what are we, teenagers?

If I've got something to say, I'll say it here, to no one.

✧

And, anyway—nights I might go out are the nights I get the kids.

Easy choice.

✦

My mom likes being able to call.

She didn't for a long time.

I don't think she wanted to talk to my wife.

They never got along.

Big surprise.

Two strong personalities.

They're actually quite alike.

.

They say you marry your mother.

.

She always said she didn't call because of my dad. Stepdad.

He kept her busy.

He has many needs.

His bad health, which has scared him into the recliner across from his TV.

Where he sits.

And mopes.

Scared about his failing body.

And the fact that he will die.

Though not for what, a dozen full years?

✧

My mom said I was busy, too, with the family, and all.

She didn't want to intrude.

She didn't want to trap the kids on the phone.

Kids hate that.

.

Only, now, I'm not married.

And I'm not that busy.

And my mother's the woman I speak to most.

.

I don't know what this all means.

✧

I don't talk to my mom nightly.

We talk once a week.

Maybe more if something's up.

If she needs to know what to buy the boy for his birthday.

If she wonders how the girl did at her swim meet.

If the TV says we got socked by bad weather.

If her dishwasher is making a noise.

Or her car.

If she thinks I should visit come Christmas.

If the kids should come, too.

If she has a question about her doctor.

If one of her friends is sick.

Or dying.

Or dead.

If she misses dad.

If she thinks I should call my brothers more.

If she's worried I'm lonely.

If she thinks leaving my wife was a bad idea, not that it's any of her business.

If she wants to remind me that marriage can be a lot of work.

If, what, I think I'm going to find someone better?

If I need to know it's no fun being alone for the rest of your life.

She imagines.

Do I?

✧

You could a fill a football stadium with what I don't know.

I don't know how to fix a dripping sink.

I don't know how to make a good omelet.

I don't know the name of the Mexican president.

Where to find Montana on a map.

I don't know how to catch fish.

Or offsides in soccer.

I don't know the difference between tripping and slashing.

I don't know how to flip turn at the end of a swim lap.

How to grow a sunflower well.

I don't know how to win video games.

I don't know math.

I don't know about Lady Gaga.

I no longer know how my computer works.

Or why I need to carry a phone all the time.

I don't know how to make small talk.

There's much I just don't know.

And I don't lose sleep over it.

So, why am I up nights?

I think my kids are mad at me.

I think they're confused.

Frightened, even.

I am.

I think I've made all the wrong decisions.

But, really, I don't know.

✧

My kids are mad at everything.

Teenager starts at twelve.

Kids funnel into the junior high building and cut loose.

The boy said, later, it was like *Lord of the Flies*.

Which my sweet girl thought sounded cool, till the boy explained.

Then she got scared, because she was next.

I said it wouldn't be bad.

I said it would be a chance to meet some new kids.

I said it would be more challenging. It would be a chance to really learn.

There would be band and newspaper and track.

What's not to like, I said.

I wasn't lying, exactly.

I gave the boy a look, and he zipped it.

Because my sweet girl didn't need to hear about the bullies and poured concrete walls.

At least not yet.

✧

Though my girl was mad her whole life, maybe.

Mad she had to leave the playground.

Or have a bath.

That the TV couldn't stay on.

Mad she had to sit in a car seat.

That she had to be in bed before her brother.

Mad that a girl at school stepped on her shoes.

That her teacher wouldn't listen to reason.

That she had to walk with her brother home.

She hated his hockey games.

Now she's mad that we don't like her friend Katie.

Mad at Katie, about something she said.

Mad she has to be home by nine.

That her parents believe R ratings mean just that.

That $150 is too much for a sweater.

That we don't understand.

That we don't trust her.

She's mad that we think she's mad.

She says she just has a keen sense of justice.

She feels its sting more than maybe anyone else.

I once suggested that justice is a relative thing.

That made her mad.

✧

For the boy it was new.

Like his dial turned to teen.

Suddenly, he had acne he hated.

Friends he hated.

School. He hated it.

Mornings. Hated.

He hated his clothes.

Hated having braces.

Hated having to talk.

Hated smiling, apparently.

My god he hated everything that came out of my mouth.

How is saying hello uncool?

And his mom and I make unreasonable requests.

Like, maybe, he should do his chores?

Really, how can we?

What do we expect from him?

He's watching TV.

He'll get to his homework.

It's not like he won't do it.

He knows how to do homework.

He's been doing it half his life.

Do we have to watch over his shoulder?

Treat him like a little kid?

.

Well.

Goddamnit.

He just was.

The day before.

A little kid.

My own little boy.

✧

Then they were mad at me.

Mad about the separation.

About my leaving.

My wife and I had argued a lot, over the years.

And nobody left.

This time I did.

The girl used the word flee.

.

They said I was quitting.

Which is not okay.

Whatever the problem.

I always said that, they said.

.

They were sort of right.

But I said some unkind words.

Which I won't repeat here.

And they were the closing lines.

.

Eventually, both kids said they understood.

Maybe they meant it.

✧

I think I need a break.

.

But I don't feel finished.

.

Maybe that's the story of my life.

✧

Other people end their marriages and move on.

Park themselves in public places.

Start conversations with strangers.

Flirt.

Maybe they find someone with whom they can have coffee.

Supper at a clean Chinese place.

They have a glass or two of wine.

Talk about music and TV.

Refer, vaguely, to their pasts.

Worry about food stuck in their teeth.

Argue over the bill.

Agree to meet again, for a movie?

They're too shy to share a goodnight kiss.

They wonder the rest of the night about what was said.

About her habit of tapping the table with the fork.

That she's pescatarian.

She's forty and never married.

That's a red flag, right?

Is a movie worth it?

Is there time for a new place to sit?

Conversation with a new stranger?

.

Christ.

How do they find the energy?

And why?

✧

Maybe you're curious.

One woman seems interested in oddballs.

Even you.

In your interests.

It's nice sitting by her.

The warm skin of her arm.

She puckers her lips a lot.

She smells like sunflower seeds.

Which is odd.

You discover she doesn't pay her parking tickets.

Her eye wanders after a glass of wine.

Which she mentions.

She knows when she's had enough.

The bottle drifts from view.

Which is funny, and not.

She likes jokes.

She asks, Why does a polar bear wear a fur coat?

She answers, Because the sweater wasn't enough.

Then laughs.

Who laughs at her own jokes?

And she likes you.

Which is altogether unlikely.

So, maybe you see why people do it.

Find someone new.

Only you're remembering your wife.

And this was twenty years ago.

✧

And even a fine thing ends in unkind words.

So, really.

Why bother?

✧

Do people think it will be different?

That they'll get on better with someone new?

That they've learned to behave.

Maybe they can't be alone.

Need someone to sit with at movies.

Or hike the southwest.

Whatever.

Maybe they need someone who can cook.

Or mow, or fix a sink.

Or make decisions.

Someone warm on the other side of the bed.

Regular sex.

Maybe they want kids.

Maybe they want more kids.

Maybe.

Maybe they're not worried it will last.

They think life's a collection of people they love and then don't.

✧

I understand the regular sex.

Only it's like every comedian says.

Marriage is the death of it.

As my wife said, I'm supposed to be in the mood after the day I've had?

I'd rather watch TV.

She said, How can I be turned on by a man who forgets to flush?

For you, she said, it's a stress reliever. For me, more stress.

You crush me, she said.

You're stinky.

Your beard scratches.

She said, Who wants someone grunting in her ear?

She said, The kids are awake.

She said, The dogs are watching.

You're not nice to me, and then you expect sex?

Forget it.

What's the point?

✧

It's no big deal, the lack of sex.

You're too tired, too.

Your knees ache on the stairs.

And you've pulled a muscle in your back.

There's that crick in your neck.

Shoulder pain.

Heartburn.

A periodic rash.

A tender ankle.

You know?

You're a wreck.

And after a morning run, and a day at work, a walk with the dog, and driving the kids around town, it seems like sleep is best.

Who doesn't like sleep?

✧

It's all the dog does, anymore.

He sleeps after breakfast, and again after our morning walk.

He sees me to the door when I leave for work, but I know he goes to sleep right after.

If I'm quiet enough coming home, I'll catch him asleep.

He sleeps after our afternoon walk, and he sleeps after his supper.

I have to roust him outside to pee before bed.

I keep buying him beds. They make him happy.

We've got one for every room. A round one. A square one. Beds with raised sides.

Of course.

He's getting old.

But he's all sorts of awake when the kids come.

He wants to play.

He begs for snacks.

Asks to be petted.

The stuff that our dog does.

So, it doesn't take a genius to see.

When it's just me, he's lonely, and bummed as hell.

✧

I suppose if someone were tending me, they'd say the same.

✧

The kids, they can be awfully attentive.

They ask, How are you feeling, Dad?

Did you sleep well, Dad?

Do you need anything, Dad?

More often than not, they want something.

Sometimes, though, they seem concerned.

Is that how you feel when your father takes up in a run-down rental? Concerned?

Are they trying to take over their mom's role—what they imagine it would be?

Do they see something in me I can't? Or won't admit?

The last possibility makes me worried.

More for their sake, than mine.

But a little bit for me.

✧

People at work say I seem tired.

They say, How are you doing?

Then, You feeling okay?

It's always the same.

.

I should ask what they mean.

Do I have bags under my eyes?

Am I greasy, unwashed?

Hunched?

Have I been staring into space?

Repeating myself?

Forgetting obligations?

What is it?

I won't ask.

They want to know about my wife and me.

They knew the first day.

I guess I had the smell of separation.

I didn't tell a single one of them.

I still haven't.

✧

I only ever talk to my friend, Andy.

He had a wife, like me.

Kids.

.

He still has the kids, some of the time.

.

He thinks of his divorce like this: A new life.

He has the house he likes.

The car he wants.

He eats what he wants, when he wants.

Sleeps on his own schedule.

In the living room, he has a little fridge full of beer.

He has a leather recliner the size of a cow.

A big-ass TV.

Weekends when the kids are with their mom, he fishes.

Evenings, he fishes.

Or he runs.

Works in his yard.

He dates divorced women who know better.

He's not in it for the commitment.

They want to have some fun, too.

.

He seems happy.

I ask if he's happy.

He says he's happy.

Why wouldn't he be happy?

✧

To Andy, I say:

You live like a teenager.

You can't do that twice.

It's your kids' turn.

Andy, I say, it's time to mind the store.

To insist on curfews.

To denounce alcohol and that demon weed.

Your kids need to do the dishes, and mow, and clean the garage.

To stick with sports, and practice piano.

They need to volunteer at the food pantry.

Stuff that builds character.

Right?

And I say, It's more than that.

If you don't read the local paper, who will?

Who will care about the county commission?

The proposed roadwork on Maple?

The budget cuts to local state parks?

This is our province, now, I say.

Our obligation.

To be adults.

To put money in college accounts.

To complain about politicians and the Facebook.

About how nothing ever changes.

Especially those damn teenagers.

Those noisy, out-of-control teenagers roaming downtown with their cigarettes and public groping. Their wisecracks and mocking looks.

Goddamit, I say to Andy, who laughs.

He thinks I'm kidding.

He asks if I want a beer.

.

Yes, I do.

✧

I tell Andy he can't ignore history.

Or he's doomed to repeat it.

He'll end up married, again.

With the same expectations.

Meaning he'll end up divorced, again, unless he's got great luck.

Divorced twice and frailer, or fatter, or both.

What's he going to do then, buy a motorcycle?

Date the old ladies at the bingo hall?

Till he gets sick of that?

And marries.

And so on?

✧

Andy doesn't listen to me.

He takes me to the bar, with his friend, Phil.

The people there, they've got their arms around each other.

And us, three guys with guts.

We're staring at young women.

One's on a stool, bent over the bar.

She seems a little excited, Andy says.

Phil says, She likes that bartender.

I say, She needs to pull up her pants. Her thong is showing.

Andy says, It's called a whale tail.

We stare.

She looks fit.

And like fun.

With her ass in the air.

She's not that much older than my sweet girl.

I hope she has friends to take her home, I say.

Or she'll end up raped in an alley.

Phil looks at the floor.

Andy looks at me.

He says I have a dark view of things.

He calls me a mope.

Fondly, of course.

He heads to the bar, to meet the bartender's friend.

Leaving poor Phil with me.

I raise my glass.

Salud.

✧

My wife took the same view.

That I'm a mope.

Though she had other names for me.

And there wasn't much fondness.

Not in the end, at least.

✧

The end.

How dramatic.

Actually, I talk to my wife every day.

Or we email.

We've even started to text, which, you know—OMG LOL ROTFL!

After all, we've got two kids to care for.

And, of late, the boy's been speaking his mind.

Which never ends well.

And the girl looks like her aunt, the pretty aunt, so there's always a boy around.

My wife says the boys are so polite, and only this far from animals.

The one at the house yesterday had a two-hour erection.

The contortions he went through to hide it. She almost felt sorry.

Boys are not allowed in my girl's room.

It's to those teenage boys that the boy's been speaking his mind.

It never ends well.

.

These are not things my wife can handle alone.

Things she doesn't want to handle alone.

Things I don't want her to handle alone.

They're *our* kids.

On this we agree.

✧

Also:

With the kids, my wife and I agree about what's okay, and what's not.

My girl's curfew.

Where she may go on dates, and where she may NOT.

And with whom.

What will happen if we find out she's broken those rules.

If she lies to us about breaking those rules.

Severe consequences, is all we're saying.

Because we don't know those older boys, and nobody feels okay about a "field party."

.

It's also understood that the boy may not use the term "J-Hole."

He may think it.

Maybe it's what we're all thinking.

About a lot of people.

Teachers, bosses, colleagues.

Maybe it's what we all call the boys hanging around at the house.

But we keep it inside.

It's *not* to come out his mouth.

Right?

Right.

✧

I called my brother a dill hole.

A scumbag. Jackwad.

I said to him, You suck raw donkey dong.

You're a peter puffer.

Captain Spankalot.

Deputy Douchebag.

Jerkweed.

Shitheel.

I called him an asswipe.

Numbnuts.

Dingleberry.

Jizz beard.

You know. The usual.

But never in front of adults.

Never *to* an adult.

The boy, on the other hand.

I think he's trying to tell us something.

✧

And he's not wrong.

We are J-Holes, most of us.

Adults, that is.

I feel like one, leaving him and his sister.

Failing their mom.

I know I'm one.

Even if I'm not sure what a J-Hole is.

✧

The kids will be in college, eventually.

In charge of themselves.

Of when to get up, or not.

What to study.

Who to know.

Soon, they'll rent apartments in frightening neighborhoods, homeless people sleeping in the entry, picking at cigarette stubs on the street, leaving urine-filled bottles like little gifts.

The smell of them an endless camping trip.

All because those apartments are a few bucks cheaper.

And since they'll be adults, they'll have to watch their money.

To start buying generic.

Pasta for every meal.

Or peanut butter.

Fewer new clothes.

The cheapest beer.

They'll drink it with people they know, and they don't.

And sleep with some of both.

Find someone to declare a boyfriend or girlfriend.

To hold hands with on campus.

To sit with at the film festival.

To bring home on vacation.

To set up house with, in a new apartment.

They'll smoke dope, late into the night.

Bare their souls.

Ignore their friends.

They'll love this person more deeply, or more differently, than anyone ever before, and feel he or she is their only future.

And end up reviling.

Break up with in public, screaming fits.

To come crying home about.

To their mother's home, and mine.

Because that's what we're here for.

Always a little more adult.

If only because we've been through it all, more than once.

✧

They already have boyfriends and girlfriends.

Something like that.

Someone they talk to on the phone.

Or text, or whatever.

Someone they might take to football games, or a dance.

Someone they have to the house for a meal.

Someone who shakes my hand and calls me Mr.

Someone exceedingly polite.

But not the same person for long.

Isn't that right?

They cycle through them kind of quick, yes?

It's all sort of innocent.

Sometime soon they'll drink some beer.

Make out at a party, or in someone's car.

They'll probably smoke a joint.

I can accept that.

I'm okay with some piercings, and maybe a tattoo.

But they won't gobble ecstasy, or shoot heroin, right?

No one's going to get his face smashed in a fight?

You hear about rape parties, and goth blood rituals.

I mean, I don't know.

You worry, especially if you don't see your children as much as you'd like.

To keep an eye on things.

To make sure they stay kids, or sort of.

Right?

✧

Because, as I've said.

They get to be kids.

I know that, at least.

There's a scene, in a film.

The father says, You'll do what I ask, because you owe me.

He says, I got up every morning, and I worked my ass off, so you could have food on the table, and so on.

And the son, brass balls and all, says back, I don't owe you shit, old man. It was your job to take care of me. Your fucking job. Don't forget it.

Probably he swore less. The old man, too.

But that's how I remember it.

Gospel.

Bring them into the world, you take care.

And don't complain.

Don't expect a thing back, except they be good to themselves.

Even if it's a shit ton of thankless grind.

Because, if ever there was a job you could love.

You know what I mean.

Now name the movie.

✧

Then, there's my life, and, if you want to help your kids, you leave, because they don't need to see you smashing the supper plates.

To hear the things I said.

To see their mom trying to punch in my face.

No one in the house could sleep.

It seemed like something worse would happen.

And I guess it did.

.

I found a new place to live.

.

But, like I said.

It's also for the best.

✧

From the first, I always told my wife time will tell.

We could decide on dinner later.

Maybe think about having a weekend at the beach.

I always said you don't buy anything on impulse.

Definitely not a car.

And who said anything about a house?

The right time for kids?

We'd know it when it came.

I said I didn't like any of those cribs.

So, why not keep our eyes open a while?

We'd find one.

What was the rush?

But she needed to know.

Always.

At twenty, she talked about retiring to California.

Or maybe the northwest.

Not Florida.

She knew about dinner, and the beach, and the car, and the house.

And the kids.

She had thoughts, at least.

And the crib?

She liked the one with the drop down side.

But there were safety issues.

And we could stand on a stool to use the other.

But it came with a cheap mattress.

So, we'd need to buy a new one.

She thought firm support would be best.

It would hold up better over time.

And she was right, about that.

She tended to be right a lot.

Except on our marriage.

She didn't see this coming.

✦

She probably knew.

You know.

That we'd split.

The inevitable end.

Being my all-seeing wife.

So, if she knew.

Then she let it happen, in a way.

She's nothing if not follow through.

Goddamn it.

That's not right.

Is it?

✧

No.

Scratch the last.

It makes no sense.

It's like blaming someone for the storm that comes.

Just because they predicted rain.

Maybe the storm stays away.

No one knows for sure.

Not even my wife.

Though she saw things more clearly than me.

Which she said a lot.

Which pissed me off.

It still pisses me off.

✧

Though I'm not by nature angry.

I'm more grouchy.

Sarcastic.

A bad example for the kids.

Even before they understood.

When they wanted to see Disney.

To which we'd have to fly.

At great cost.

And the hotel?

And the park passes?

The meals?

For a week?

Sure.

We didn't need to fix the car.

Or eat for a few months.

Here's what we needed:

To mill around with sweaty people clutching cameras.

We needed to stand in line and stand and stand, and then ride a ride for two minutes, and repeat.

Amusement park food?! Bring on the ketchup!

I said, I'm all for structured fun. I bet they have "evening activities" for the kids. I want a hostess who reads a bedtime tale into her mic!

And the uniformed employees with their sincere smiles and well wishes!

The thought of getting hugged by big Mickey!

It gave me the shivers, it did, and I said so!

I made us all feel bad.

Even the kids, who understood my tone.

.

That settled it.

Because my wife would be damned if I'd ruin everyone's fun.

They want to go, she said.

So, we're going to go, she said.

Do you hear me?

Sure, I said.

And we went.

And it was a lot of fun.

Really.

I mean it.

✧

I learned.

Vacations.

Families take them. A couple a year.

You don't sit around the house, reading.

Or watching TV.

You plan.

And charge deposits to your card.

You schedule a dog sitter.

Talk about your excitement.

You pack your bags.

Spend an airless day in the hum of a car.

Or a plane.

Or both.

And, then.

Well.

Vacations are fun.

I learned.

Who doesn't like lounging around a cottage by the beach?

Turning the AC to subarctic.

Sleeping late.

Then swimming.

Or hiking up the hot, sliding sands of a dune.

Riding the rides.

Calamari lightly breaded with a drizzle of oil.

Drinking dirty martinis.

You might even kid around with your kids.

Who behave, because they're happy.

Happy like your wife.

Who holds your hand.

.

Leave your computer home.

Along with complaints about the cost.

And every other lousy thing in your life.

.

Which, you know.

You're just putting off.

Don't kid yourself.

It doesn't last.

✧

So, what?

Nothing lasts.

Life comes in waves.

And.

And I say you take the good.

You take the bad.

You take them both.

And there you have.

The facts of life.

The facts of life.

.

My shrink asks why I make jokes.

Does it help to make fun of things?

She has the patience of a saint.

And a surprising memory about crappy TV.

✧

What did you think?

I accept my life?

Think again.

Once a week I sit in a roomful of dusty plants, in an armchair kitty-corner to Dr. Levan, who folds her legs and yawns behind her hand.

I talk.

And she listens.

Asks questions.

Advises.

And I talk.

And so on.

.

And this.

Which she says I shouldn't think of as homework.

Just work I do at home.

More therapy.

So I can understand.

.

I've asked her what I should hope to understand.

She says that's a good question:

What do I hope to understand?

✧

I'll tell you what I want to know.

I want to know what comes next.

INVENTORY

This house had sheets in the closet, dishes in the cabinets. Out back, a cord of wood.

There were bicycles in the garage. Children in the bedrooms. Tall, messy, attractive children who put on confused looks at the sight of her, no matter how often they saw her.

Because she wasn't theirs.

And they weren't hers.

She came with a car, which she parked in an open space in the garage, and she brought clothes for a weekend, a box with soap and toothpaste, a hair dryer. She had her briefcase. A laptop. Some jewelry. She brought a few photos stuffed in a folder she found in the basement of her old home. The folder—a portfolio, really— had belonged to one of her own children, though which one she couldn't say. She remembered buying it a half-dozen years before. She remembered how someone had wanted it so very much.

Its fabric was frayed at the corners. The zipper stopped short of closing, leaving a hole like a wound.

She brought as keepsakes the stuffed animals she still kept, though she was a woman in her forties, wide in the hips and thick across her stomach. She'd certainly forgotten something important, but she wasn't worried. Why worry?

For now it was hard enough finding room for herself, figuring out where on the sofa she belonged, or where at the dinner table, and how she should flatten herself against the wall when this man's kids pushed through. She didn't know if she had a right to the remote. She didn't know if she should move a magazine from the table so she could set down her coffee. She didn't know where she would drop her purse on coming home, or if she could call it home, at all. It was, to be sure a house (noun), the usual residence of a person, family, or household. It was not, however, the place in which one's domestic affections were centered.

Not.

Except in the bedroom, where this man had more than cleared a dresser and closet—had, instead, started fresh, down to the new rails run under the box spring, which was new, like the mattress, and the sheets, and the comforter, the headboard and dressers and dressing table and chair in the corner. The armoire. A bedroom suite, he said, wanting to say something more—she could see—but he didn't, just smiled. She pushed off her shoes and sat on the bed, then lowered, slowly, back. Closed her eyes. Said it was nice. Very nice. And thank you.

Only he was still there, standing at the foot of the bed, and then sitting, when she thought he had turned to go out. He had the sense to stay quiet, though she knew he was watching her, which made it hard to feel the new quilt under her back or the warmth of the room, or to hear the way the walls muted sounds from the rest of the house. She couldn't concentrate on the breath fluting through her nose. It was all just him, waiting, his weight making the mattress shift. She held out her hand, hoping it would be enough, and let the knot in her stomach loosen, and wondered how many beds a person knows in her life.

For her, for her childhood, just one bed, with a headboard painted in thick, grainy strokes by her father, and a mattress that went soft as an old apple by the time she moved on. Changed. To the dorm pallets stuffed with batting, over wire-mesh springs. Then the futon in her apartment, and the one in her boyfriend's. And the next boyfriend's. And the next. They all ended up flattened to nothing and pitted where people slept, the futons did. How excited the last boyfriend was when the money from their marriage—the gifts—made enough for a mattress, a real one, which they moved, after a while, into a house of their own. She had been excited, too—but more when they bought another, and then another, for the children. How many nights had she ended up asleep on those, after reading her kids one book, then two, then three?

Those kids with their father, now, and her here, hearing the air hum from a vent. She said to this man that she needed a few minutes, then she'd be out. She said maybe they should take his kids for some food. He should decide where to go. Anywhere was fine. She just needed a minute. Then she'd be out. Just a minute.

Though, to be true, twenty or thirty more years of her life would not be time enough, no matter how thoughtful this man, or how funny his smile. The silver in his eyebrows. The dimple in his ear where a stud once went. His loud, harmless kids would not be enough. Their messes. This neighborhood canopied by old oaks dropping their seeds into grass tended by young men on mowers. It would not be enough. Nor would the neighbors in shorts and short-sleeved shirts and sandals. The dogs in yards. The quiet air after evening. None of it. Not the restaurant the man would choose, or a glass of wine, or weekends with his kids at soccer games in fields lined by fall leaves. Not walks. Not the fire in the fireplace, or a movie, the two of them, or the car ride there and back, in the already dark evening. Not the way the man settled between her legs, his cheek on her neck. Not bicycle rides. Not a week of vacation, at the beach, with its hot sand. Not the shaded deck off the cottage they would rent, or the warm wind. Not the pleasure of others around her, or their love, or anger, sadness. Not even those things.

Because it was years since she felt afraid of her father's cracked voice. Or the wholeness of her mother's lap. Since she wanted a sister whose hair she could comb, or a brother to pull in a cart. Since crying was something she couldn't control.

Because it was years since she grew apart from her first friends. Years since the small sadness of that. Years since she thrilled at the gift of a nail kit. Since she wanted a dog small enough to carry. Since she had to have a blue dress like her mother's. Years since she found satisfaction shaving her legs. Since she passed someone a note. A note on lined paper folded into eighths. Years since one boy took her to the movies and held her hand until it sweated slick. Since she could remember his name. Years since she imagined she could flee her parents. Since she could imagine places that would be new. The small city of her college, with shops and bars, people always wandering on the downtown streets. Years from nights she dressed to go for drinks.

It was years since she took a job because it allowed her to move south. Since she felt thrilled on an airplane's leaving the ground. Or holding the metal rod on a subway car as it leaned through a turn. Years since the gym-shiny wood floors of her own first house, when she and her husband paid men to wrap their furniture in padded blankets and help them move in. How she and her husband had tilled the dirt backyard before spreading fertilizer and seed and straw, then watered. Since she remembered that. How hot it was. How anxious they'd been to do it right. How they'd left one corner for a vegetable garden. How they'd planted flowers in lines along the fence. She remembered every inch of that day. And then the way her breasts stretched full with pregnancy, and hours of labor in the room made dark by painkillers and—still—such pain.

She felt so afraid those babies would die. She couldn't even make a tomato ripen in the compost-black soil and fat heat of their summers.

Years since so little sleep she could drift off sitting. Since once she woke to the baby boy feeding her a limp spider husk.

Since memories were memorable.

Even every day for years washing clothes and walking a dog and shopping and cooking macaroni and cheese and cheese macaroni and noodles with cheese sauce for the girl. Driving from home to daycare to work to daycare to home.

And it had been so hard to say that the son couldn't bounce a basketball on the living-room floor, and she gathered him up as he cried at the injustice of it, and everyone in the house had to know what was wrong.

The sick duck sound of a trumpet long since abandoned.

Since one more too-loud TV show would strip open her nerves, making her scream until her throat folded.

Since she and the man and the kids spent hours and hours in the car on vacation. That tight, airless little space.

Since the boy and girl hugged into the fold of her body, and how much they loved her.

She knows they still do, but some part of it is lost.

Faded.

How present they were in their life all happening every minute.

The girl so anxious to win the spelling bee, but failing out in the first round, and crying, and crying.

When her boy was almost the age of the boys in this house, off to his first dance in a midnight blue suit and such a wide leather belt and shoes with such thick heels. Her husband said, We've raised a pimp.

How she had laughed and gone to bed that night feeling her life couldn't be more full, and that it would soon be done.

Done but not over.

She sat up, opened her eyes. She called to this man that she was coming. Said she was sorry for being so slow. Said it to the room. She stood. Tugged the bottom of her blouse. Found her shoes. Called again, imagining her voice lost in arguments about what, restaurants? Who would sit in the back of the car?

What she heard in return was the pulse in her throat. The soft burr of carpet underfoot.

She heard herself call again. Waited.

She imagined her voice drowned under the clatter of kids getting shoes.

People, moving.

But she heard none of that.

She heard nothing, not this man's voice or the sound of his kids. The house was hushed, as if asleep, or in shock, blanketed by the winter's worst snow. Only it was summer, and she was sweating, suddenly, under her arms and down her back. She felt surprised. And surprised to feel afraid, of all things.

She'd taken too long. They'd grown tired of waiting for a silly, slow woman. Or they'd forgotten she'd come, at all, and had gone about their business, like they'd done the day before and the one before that.

But there was no doing that. How could anyone do that? This man couldn't. The children wouldn't.

They wouldn't have left. Not without her.

They were there, she knew.

They were there, in the foyer, in a half circle, frozen, senses trained on the hall she would have to enter and pass through. Waiting. Wondering, just like her, on this side of the door.